Jasper has not been idle since the night he committed the corpse of his brother to the watery bosom of the Bast. He has called in many favours and brought certain pressures to bear. Jasper Pepper is a surprisingly influential man, and the power he exercises over those who share his unconventional beliefs is considerable.

Jasper stares at the poster, certain that he has discovered a vital clue, but a vital clue to what? He sighs, knowing that he has come to the limits of what human knowledge can offer him. Further investigation will involve robes, a pentagram, and a considerable quantity of blood . . .

THE BLACK SPHINX

Matt Hart

CORGI BOOKS

THE BLACK SPHINX
A CORGI BOOK
978 0552 55421 3 (from January 2007)
0 552 55421 9

Published in Great Britain by Corgi Books,
an imprint of Random House Children's Books

This edition published 2006

1 3 5 7 9 10 8 6 4 2

Papers used by Random House Children's Books are
natural, recyclable products made from wood grown
in sustainable forests. The manufacturing processes
conform to the environmental regulations of the
country of origin.

Set in 12/19pt Gioconda by
Falcon Oast Graphic Art Ltd.

Corgi Books are published by
Random House Children's Books,
61–63 Uxbridge Road, London W5 5SA,
a division of The Random House Group Ltd,
in Australia by Random House Australia (Pty) Ltd,
20 Alfred Street, Milsons Point, Sydney, NSW 2061, Australia,
in New Zealand by Random House New Zealand Ltd,
18 Poland Road, Glenfield, Auckland 10, New Zealand,
and in South Africa by Random House (Pty) Ltd,
Isle of Houghton, Corner Boundary Road & Carse O'Gowrie,
Houghton 2198, South Africa

THE RANDOM HOUSE GROUP Limited Reg. No. 954009
www.kidsatrandomhouse.co.uk

A CIP catalogue record for this book is
available from the British Library.

Printed and bound in Great Britain by
Bookmarque Ltd, Croydon, Surrey

For Tim and Vicky,
with love

Chapter One
Death in the Particular

This is Wolveston on a filthy February night. The city is held fast in the grip of one of the smogs known as 'a Wolveston particular'. The sulphurous air is so thick and grey that breathing it in is like inhaling fleece. The smog hangs thickest over the grey-green waters of the River Bast. Along the Embankment, the glowing globes of the gaslights resemble smeared angels.

The streets of the capital are singularly quiet, for a particular has to be treated with respect. 'If you gets a particular down on yer chest,' as a popular saying goes, 'you're a goner for sure!'

But here is a man who has chosen to ignore such warnings. He is a tall man, lanky, a toff by the look of his fur-collared coat and shiny opera hat. His face is heavily whiskered, as is the fashion among the fashionable, but a close inspection would reveal that his apparently black whiskers have been dyed an unconvincing shade of purple. His coat is made of shoddy and the fur of its collar is rabbit. In short, he is a fake gentleman with a pale face that is slick with sweat. His name is Malachi Pepper and he recently celebrated his fiftieth birthday; he will not live to celebrate his fifty-first.

Malachi walks briskly, and though he does not turn his head, he is listening intently for following footsteps. He passes the red marble statue of an eagle, a monument presented to the nation by a grateful America, which was granted independence in 1773 following a nasty incident involving tea and Boston harbour.

This had threatened to develop into a war but was brought to a peaceful resolution by the diplomatic skills of Chief Minister Lavering. There is an inscription on the plinth of the statue, TALK TO ME OF LIBERTY, OR TALK TO ME OF DEATH! but the badly carved eagle does not seem to be about to talk of either. In fact the statue inspires so little awe that shortly after its erection, some wag christened it Pretty Polly and so it has been known ever since.

Malachi leaves the Embankment and crosses into St George's Lane, which leads on to the edge of Parliament Park. Though the smog obscures the towers, spires and domes of the Parliament building, Malachi can feel its presence, like the scowl of a disapproving uncle. He pauses at a squat blue postbox, and here he does look behind and all around him. There is no one there. Malachi deftly withdraws an envelope from within his coat and slips it into the open mouth of the box like a mother bird feeding its chick. Then he retraces his steps down St George's Lane. His manner has changed. He now walks with the light, easy gait of a man who has just relieved himself of an onerous burden – which he has. Though the air is foul, in his mind he sees fair weather and happy days ahead. He feels that he is in his prime, and that his real life has begun at last.

Back on the Embankment, Malachi descends Greyfriars Stairs to a jetty and he is in luck, for here is a rowing boat with a lantern at its prow, and in the boat sits a ferryman, wrapped in a cloak, with a felt hat on his head. The brim of the hat is so broad and floppy that its edges almost touch his shoulders, and the only part of his face that is visible is an inch or so of bristly chin.

'Ho there, fellow!' says Malachi. 'How much to row me to Chesterfield Wharf?'

'A shilling, skipper,' the ferryman replies.

This seems reasonable to Malachi and he makes as if to step into the boat.

'In advance,' growls the ferryman.

Malachi laughs at the man's insolence, digs into a trouser pocket, finds a silver coin and holds it out. The ferryman accepts it and helps Malachi aboard.

The middle of the river in a smog is a curious place to be. There is no Wolveston, just the two men, the boat, the sloshing water and the creaking of the oars.

'Got far to go, skipper?' enquires the ferryman.

'Pretty far,' Malachi says, and he means it, for Chesterfield Wharf lies near to Grand Metropolitan Station. From there he intends to catch a train to Dover, a steam packet to Calais, and after that he will disappear among Europe's teeming millions. These last few dangerous months have demanded constant vigilance and

Malachi's greatest ambition is to be a nobody, a person of no account who attracts no attention.

Without a word of explanation, the ferryman suddenly ships his oars.

'What are you about?' Malachi demands. 'I paid you to row, so row, damn your eyes!'

The ferryman flicks his right hand, and a derringer appears in it. The little pistol clicks twice as the ferryman cocks its hammer with his thumb.

Malachi is too flabbergasted to be alarmed. 'What d'you think you're doing?'

In a voice quite different to the one he used previously, the ferryman says, 'Where is it, Malachi?'

Fear comes to Malachi. His chest thumps with it, his mouth is sour with the taste of it. His horrified stare turns his eyes to billiard balls. 'You!' he gasps.

'Quite so.'

'But how did you know where to find me?'

6

'No great feat,' says the ferryman. 'You're a creature of habit, Malachi. It's always been a serious weakness of yours. Every evening, come rain or shine, you take the same constitutional stroll that fetches you to Greyfriars Stairs and a boat across the river. The only difference is that tonight I've contrived to be your boatman. I say again – where is it?'

Malachi swallows. 'Where's what? I don't know what you're talking about.'

The ferryman groans. 'Oh do grow up, Malachi!' he scolds. 'You were just like this at school. *Please, sir, it wasn't me, sir! I didn't do anything, sir!* It was pathetic then and it's still pathetic now. Have some respect for your own intelligence, if not for mine.'

Malachi has registered little of this, so deeply is he concentrating on the muzzle of the gun. 'I haven't got it,' he says evasively.

'Then where is it?'

'Somewhere no one will find it,' says Malachi. He nods at the derringer. 'Why don't you put that away? We both know that you can't afford to kill me.'

'Perhaps not,' the ferryman replies, 'but death isn't the worst I have to offer, Malachi. My studies have made me an expert in certain obscure but effective methods of interrogation. You can avoid all manner of unpleasantness by telling me the object's whereabouts.'

Malachi's mind works furiously, exploring possibilities and following them through to their consequences. 'You are the last person I'd tell,' he declares.

The ferryman smiles. 'That can be very easily arranged.'

Malachi's inner tension explodes into outward action. He lunges at the ferryman, who half stands to repel the attack. They lock in a tussle while the boat yaws beneath them. A small portion of the River Bast slops over the rocking gunwale. The men grimace and grunt, holding each other in a tight embrace. Their mutual hatred has drawn them as close as lovers.

There is a loud report. Malachi's arms drop to his sides and the ferryman steps away from him. Glancing down at his chest, Malachi sees a wound that has never been there before. He gazes glassily at the ferryman, whispers, 'Jasper?' then his knees buckle and he tumbles backwards into the river.

The ferryman sits down heavily and curses Malachi in a long string of ingenious phrases. When he reaches the string's end, he recovers his presence of mind. The only link between him and Malachi's death is the derringer, and he pitches it over the side. He has got away with murder before, and does not doubt that he will get away with it again this time. There is no denying that things have gone badly though. A carefully prepared plan has missed its main object, but the ferryman is determined. Nothing and no one is going to come between him and what he wants.

He thinks, and thinks, and thinks.

CHAPTER TWO
A CHANGE

On the afternoon of the following day, some one hundred and thirty miles away from Wolveston, Crispin Rattle is seated on a stool outside Latimer's dry goods store, weaving a reed basket. Crispin is twelve years old, curly-haired, pale-faced, freckled, snub-nosed, grey-eyed, thin as a rail and so tall for his age that he may well have outgrown his strength. Above him, the sky is black and threatening; all around him lies London.

Somewhere between a village and a town, London is a place that time has passed by, as have wealth, industry and beauty. Most of its inhabitants dwell in thatched cottages, in the back yards of which some keep their pigs and poultry. Most of its trade, via the River Thames, is with its larger neighbours, Maidenhead and Reading. Most of its populace is poor, as Crispin's family is.

Basket weaving is not a full-time job and Crispin will be paid no more than a pittance for his work, but things being what they are in London, even a pittance will be a welcome addition to the income his parents earn at Warren's boot-blacking factory. Though young, Crispin Rattle is something of a jack of all trades and has cheerfully and uncomplainingly turned his hand to hop picking, potato gathering and eel catching. As his fingers nimbly twist the reeds, he is vaguely aware of the sound of approaching boots, but when those boots stop directly before him, he looks up into the plump, bewhiskered face of Constable Cudlip of the Essex County Constabulary.

'You Rattle, Crispin?' says the constable.

'Yes, sir,' Crispin says.

'Son of Rattle, Oliver, and Rattle, Rachel?'

'Yes, sir,' Crispin says, feeling increasingly concerned.

'I'm sorry to inform you that there's been an accident at the blacking factory,' says Constable Cudlip. 'Your parents are no more.'

Rain spatters the pavement, lightning crackles, thunder rolls; Crispin's life changes for ever.

To Crispin, a week of solid rain appears to ensue, a week of clouds and dinginess. After the first sharp pain and tears, a horrible numb emptiness takes hold of him. He sleeps, wakes, eats and cannot understand the point of any of these activities. The local vicar calls, but Crispin soon sends him on his way. The man and his religion are strangers to him. If Crispin was inclined to believe in God, which he is not, he would rail against the deity for making him an orphan, but that slender comfort is not afforded to him. The loss of his parents, though keenly felt, does not form part of some greater plan.

A small event greatly upsets Crispin. A letter arrives for his mother, one of a number of letters she began to receive in the summer, and whose contents she kept a close secret. That the unknown correspondent should be ignorant of her death strikes Crispin as somehow unfair. Why should this person be alive while his mother is dead? He rages for a while against this injustice, then stops, for his anger is as meaningless as his own existence seems to him. He leaves the letter unopened on the mantelpiece.

On the day of his parents' funeral, it rains. Crispin follows the donkey-drawn parish cart and feels ashamed of the shoddily made coffins that it bears.

The ceremony and interment take place in a doleful corner of St Paul's churchyard. St Paul's itself is pretty doleful, mean, mossy and messy, leaky-guttered. The weather vane fell from its tower years ago and the roof is in urgent need of re-slating. Crispin would have preferred there to be no ceremony, but it cannot be avoided. The vicar chants the customary rhythmic platitudes. Crispin throws the first handful of earth down onto the coffins and shudders at the noise it makes. The gravedigger steps forward with his spade held at the ready, and the affair is done with.

Or perhaps not quite done with, for as Crispin follows the path that leads to the churchyard gate, he is surprised to see Lucan Treddle coming in the opposite direction. Lucan Treddle is a publican and the Rattles' landlord. Under the impression that the man has come to pay his respects to his deceased tenants, Crispin is touched, but does not remain so for long.

'Afternoon, Mr Treddle, sir,' Crispin says politely.

'Afternoon?' rasps Lucan Treddle. 'Afternoon! I'll give you afternoon, you brassy young pup! You've got a nerve to speak to me at all.'

Crispin cannot account for the landlord's hostility, until Lucan Treddle says, 'You've been living rent-free in my property for over a week, and that's long enough. I'm a businessman, not a charity. I want you out of the house by noon tomorrow, understand?'

'But where will I go, Mr Treddle?' Crispin exclaims.

'Damned if I know, damned if I care,' replies Lucan Treddle. 'Go to your relatives.'

'Ain't got none, Mr Treddle, sir,' Crispin says.

'Then go to the devil!' says Lucan Treddle. 'Noon tomorrow – remember!'

* * *

That evening, Crispin Rattle strikes the last match in the house, lights the last candle and reviews his future prospects. They are not promising. He is hungry, cold, and has no one in the world to care for him except himself. The parish orphanage, a dreadful place where starving children tease lengths of ships' rope into oakum until their fingernails are broken and bleeding, beckons to him, but Crispin would rather throw himself into the Thames. A life of crime has its appeal, though Crispin cannot seriously imagine himself offering violence to anyone, and he knows that he is too clumsy to steal without being caught. He has two shillings and ninepence to his name, and in eighteen hours he will be homeless. Dark thoughts crowd in on him like flocks of bats.

Then Crispin recalls the letter and, despite himself, he feels a glimmer of hope. Perhaps the person who wrote it was kindly disposed towards his mother and might, in turn, be kindly disposed towards him. He takes the letter down from the mantelpiece, opens the envelope and unfolds the sheet of paper inside. His forehead crinkles into a deep frown as he reads:

K B Z L O K D K C F E H L
D P J V T L C Y P A D G N
I V A Z X K T E P G E C N

For a moment the letter and the world become ludicrous, and Crispin begins to giggle, but his mirth is cut short as a gentle, impossible voice says, 'Crispin?'

Crispin turns his head and sees Rachel Rattle. She is wearing the grey shift that she was buried in. Her face is blueish, her lips are the colour of earthworms.

'Ma?' Crispin gasps. 'What you doing here? I thought you was dead.'

'I'm as dead as nails,' says Rachel. 'Listen to me, Crispin, I haven't got long. Leave London. Go to Wolveston. Find Callisto. You remember what I told you about Callisto?'

'Yes, Ma,' Crispin says.

'Find him and show him the letter, Crispin,' urges Rachel. 'You can trust him. He'll help and protect you.'

'I'll find him, Ma, I promise,' Crispin says. 'Are you a ghost?'

'I suppose I must be,' Rachel says.

'I always thought I'd be afraid of ghosts, but I ain't afraid of you.'

'There are plenty of things to fear in this world, but not my ghost,' says Rachel. 'I chose you because you've got a good heart.'

Crispin is flummoxed.

'Chose me for what, Ma?' he says. 'I don't understand.'

There is much that Crispin does not understand, such as how this can be happening, and why his mother seems partly not herself, and partly someone who she never was.

Rachel half turns her head, as if she hears her name being called. 'I'll come to you again, Crispin, but I must go now.'

'Aw, d'you have to, Ma?' Crispin grumbles. 'Can't you—?'

He is alone again.

Until this moment, Crispin has put no faith in ghosts or any kind of afterlife, and he estimates that the time is not right for him to reconsider the ins and outs of his philosophy. In life, Rachel Rattle was a canny, practical woman who gave canny, practical advice, and it appears that the grave has not diminished those qualities.

Wolveston – why not? thinks Crispin. I'll be better off in Wolveston than if I stick around here. No one ever found his fortune in London.

CHAPTER THREE
A MATINÉE PERFORMANCE

This is Wolveston on a late afternoon in March. The sun is low in the west. Its cement-coloured light silhouettes the great pyramids that stand on Cromwell Hill, forming the Wolveston Necropolis. Within each pyramid the remains of the dearly departed lie in compartments sealed by steel doors shut fast with combination locks to prevent interference by creatures of the night or practitioners of the occult.

At the heart of the city the sunlight gleams on the gilded statues of the four lions that guard the rooftop of the Commonwealth Bank, into whose vaults untold wealth pours from all over the globe, and pretty much stays put. The bank stands at one end of Commercial Road, which at its other end meets at a junction with Broadway, the most famous street in the most famous city in the world. Walk down Broadway and you will hear every language known to humanity. It is a street of grand shops, hotels and restaurants, cafés, theatres and museums, a street that never sleeps, a street that is always glamorous, even when it rains.

Crispin Rattle wanders through the crowds. The denizens of Broadway eye the boy askance – and little wonder, for he is a woeful spectacle. His clothes are shabby, his boots are cracked and worn through at the soles. The peak of his cap is half torn off. There is mud on his cheeks, in his hair, on his boots. It has taken him weeks to get to the city, and there were times when only his conversations with his dead mother kept him going. She has guided and consoled him continually. In an odd way, Crispin feels closer to his mother now than he did when she was alive. In another, odder way he feels more distant. Perhaps fatigue and hunger have affected his mind, but there are times when Crispin could swear that he hears another voice inside Rachel's, and sees another shape inside her shape.

Crispin is unaware of the distaste that he provokes in the people he passes, for he is in a kind of daze. He has never been among buildings so tall and grand, and has consequently never felt himself to be so small and humble. It is his first visit to Wolveston, and the metropolis has over-whelmed him.

About halfway along Broadway, Crispin stops in front of a curious building, Tuttleby and Hawker's Egyptian Hall. Its entrance doors are flanked by a pair of fluted pillars that support a lintel on which two lion-headed human figures in their turn support an arch. The building's oblong windows are framed in stone carved with all manner of symbols and hieroglyphs. A poster on display announces:

MESSERS TUTTLEBY & HAWKER
ARE PROUD TO PRESENT
CALLISTO
Master of Magic and Illusion

Crispin's shoulders sag with weariness. He has found what he came to Wolveston to find, and the relief brings him close to tears. When he attempts to enter the hall, however, he finds his way barred by a bulky doorman in a maroon coat trimmed with gold braid.

'What's your game, squib?' the doorman barks.

'I ain't playing no game, sir,' says Crispin. 'I want to go inside and see Mr Callisto.'

'I expect you do,' the doorman says, 'but have you got a ticket?'

'No, sir,' confesses Crispin. 'But I got an important message for Mr Callisto from an old friend of his.'

'Messenger-boys use the stage door entrance,' the doorman says huffily. He points. 'Go down there, take your first left into Paradise Lane. You'll know the stage door when you see it – it's done up like a mummy's tomb.'

Crispin thanks the doorman and goes on his way.

The Egyptian Hall is a place of mystery both without and within, for although it is a theatre, it is not a place where dramas are presented. This is the high temple of British conjuring, illusion and magic. Inside its walls, the impossible becomes possible and audiences generally leave boggle-eyed and open-mouthed. Upon its stage miracles occur on a daily basis, with matinées at weekends. And since it *is* the weekend, just such a matinée is about to reach its finale, for Callisto is performing.

He stands centre-stage in a pool of lime-light. He is dressed formally in a black swallow-tailed jacket and a stiff-fronted white shirt with a black bow tie fastened around its collar. His face is long, his eyes are green, his hair is dark. There is something of the wolf in his lopsided smile, something of the cat in his graceful movements.

Beside him is a young girl, his assistant Aril. Aril is doe-eyed, sloe-eyed and brown-skinned. She wears baggy trousers of scarlet silk and a glittering short-sleeved top.

Callisto snaps his fingers in front of Aril's face. Her eyelids flutter and close. The orchestra in the pit strikes up a writhing, sinuous melody. A stage hand wheels on a packing trunk from the wings.

Callisto unfastens and unhasps the trunk, opens its many flaps, drawers and doors, and raps it with his knuckles. The trunk is empty and sounds hollow. The magician seals it up again and turns his – and the audience's – attention back to his assistant. He makes a gesture. Aril stiffens and tilts backwards, as straight and stiff as a poker, pivoting until her head is no more than a metre from the stage. Callisto circles his hands around her. Aril responds by moving so that her heels leave the stage. She is lying on her back, suspended in the air, and slowly rises until she is level with Callisto's chest. From nowhere he produces a hoop of bright metal which he passes over Aril several times, to demonstrate that she is not supported on wires. Then he bends down and appears to whisper in her ear.

Aril floats up and up, and drifts as gently as a bubble into the auditorium, high above the audience. The orchestra falls silent except for the drummer, who begins a long roll. Keeping time with the drummer, Aril spins, head over feet, feet over head, getting faster and faster until she's a blur. Sparks fountain from her fingers and toes, surrounding her in smoke and fire. There is a bright greenish flash, an explosion that draws cries of alarm from several spectators, and the smoke clears to reveal nothing. The beautiful young girl has disappeared, a victim, it seems, of spontaneous combustion.

There is an atmosphere of shock in the theatre, and an anger that directs itself at Callisto. What kind of fiend is it who would destroy a sweet and innocent child simply in order to entertain the public?

Callisto's smile grows even more lopsided. With astonishing rapidity he opens up the trunk...and Aril steps out of it. Callisto takes her by the hand and they both bow as the audience applauds wildly, gets to its feet, showers the stage with flowers and handkerchiefs, and hoarsely shouts, 'Bravo!'

A little later Callisto is in his dressing room, seated before a large mirror. He is using a piece of cloth and a jar of hand-cream to remove his stage make-up. The door of the dressing room is open, and he receives a stream of well-wishers and admirers, and a group of three young men who neither admire him nor wish him well. They are blades, toffed-up to the nines, squiffy with drink and eager to have a cheap laugh at someone else's expense. One, who can bray more loudly than his companions, says, 'Top-hole show, Callisto, top hole!'

'I'm pleased that you enjoyed it,' Callisto replies.

'That last trick,' the young man blusters on, 'when you made the girl go bang – where did you pick that up, from a fakir?'

'Satan taught it to me, the night that I sold him my soul,' says Callisto.

The young men's laughter sounds like plates shattering on flagstones.

'Don't your daughter mind being blown to kingdom come?' demands the young man.

He has gone too far. Muscles twitch in Callisto's jaw as he says, 'She's not my daughter. I'm her guardian,' and his voice is low, even, dangerous.

The young man frowns. 'Guardian – to an oriental? How did that come about – did you buy her in a bazaar?'

Callisto turns in his chair and fixes the young man's gaze with his own. 'That's a story that must remain untold until I judge that the world is ready for it,' he says. 'And now I believe that you've taken up enough of my time, so I bid you good day.'

The young man is offended. His blood is up and he means to pick a fight, but just as he is about to snarl an insult, he notices something in Callisto's eyes that makes him realize that he knows the man, has known him all his life. Callisto is the monster that used to lurk in the nursery bedroom dark; he is the nameless, shapeless beast that pursues him through glaring nightmares. The young man blinks. The solid, everyday world around him threatens to split open and reveal another kind of reality. 'I, er!' he jabbers. 'I, er! I, er!'

His friends lead him away.

Callisto returns to the mirror and catches the reflection of half a face peeping round the edge of the door. He grunts impatiently and says, 'Can I be of any assistance?'

'I hope so, sir,' says a voice.

Crispin Rattle appears in the doorway, holding a threadbare cap that he twists as though he were wringing it out.

Without knowing why, Callisto takes an instant liking to the boy. There is something sweet about him that contrasts strongly with the sourness of Callisto's last encounter.

The magician's manner softens. 'And who might you be, young man?' he asks.

'Please, sir,' says the boy, 'I'm—!' and he faints dead away.

Chapter Four
The Message

It seems to Crispin Rattle that he has tripped over and is falling away from the world, down a vast well of blackness. And then he is somehow falling upwards, and the world returns to him as gradually as dawn breaking. First he hears a noise, a huge voice that echoes in his ears, speaking in an apparently foreign tongue.

'Are you all right?'

Crispin cannot understand. He groans like a creaking door.

'Here, drink this.'

A cold rim presses against Crispin's lips. He takes a swallow of a liquid that draws a long, hot comet-tail from his throat to his belly and makes him cough. His eyes open. He is in Callisto's dressing room, lying on the floor. The master magician himself is supporting his shoulders. Someone else is present too, an exotic-looking girl whose eyes are as dark and deep as the well that Crispin saw himself plunge into. She has trousers on, and boots, and a collarless shirt. Why is she wearing men's clothes?

Crispin coughs again.

'Steady!' says Callisto. 'If I give you a hand, do you think you can sit in a chair?'

Crispin nods. Callisto hauls him upright and assists him into the chair in front of the mirror.

'When did you last eat?' asks Callisto.

'S morning, sir,' Crispin says.

'And what did you eat?'

'Bit of pie crust, sir.'

Callisto growls.

'It was all I could get, sir!' says Crispin,

sounding apologetic. 'I didn't have no money to get nothing else.'

Callisto conjures up half a loaf of bread, a wedge of cheese and a tankard of milk and tells Crispin to eat. Crispin is uncomfortably aware that Callisto and the girl are watching, but he is too hungry to let the awareness inhibit him, and he dispatches the food with a will.

'Feel a little better?' says Callisto, when the boy has finished.

'Yes thank you, sir!' says Crispin, putting a hand to his mouth to suppress a belch.

'Good,' says Callisto. 'By the look of those boots, you've done some travelling recently. What's your name and where are you from?'

'My name's Crispin, sir. Crispin Rattle. I'm from London.'

'London?' says Callisto, puzzled. 'London?' Then he places it: a quiet market town on the River Thames, noted chiefly for its Goose Fair and hobbyhorses. 'What does a London boy want in Wolveston?'

'To see you about this, sir,' comes the reply. Crispin slips his hand inside his jacket and brings out an envelope which he hands to Callisto.

Callisto gives the envelope a swift glance that registers the date of the Wolveston postmark and the address.

Mrs Rachel Rattle
5, ST PETER'S LANE
LONDON
ESSEX

'A relative of yours?' Callisto says.

'My ma, sir,' says Crispin. 'Only the letter didn't come till after she died, her and my pa together. They was killed in a blacking factory accident.'

'Oh, you poor thing!' Aril exclaims.

It is the first time that Crispin has heard her speak. He knows that he ought to thank her, but when he tries, his face blushes a fiery red and the words will not leave his mouth. Only when he talks to Callisto can he find his voice. 'Please to look inside, sir,' he says.

Callisto retrieves a small sheet of paper from the envelope. On it is inscribed:

K B Z L O K D K C F E H L
D P J V T L C Y P A D G N
I V A Z X K T E P G E C N

'Is it writ in Russian, sir?' Crispin enquires.

'No, it's gibberish,' says Callisto, 'or it's in code. What made you bring it to me?'

'Ma did,' Crispin says. 'She always reckoned...' Tears well up in Crispin's eyes. He wipes his nose with the back of his left hand and sniffs. 'She said as how you was a great one for puzzles and mysteries and such, and that you was the cleverest bloke she know'd of.'

'She knew me?' Callisto says, astonished.

'When you was both a bit younger, sir,' says Crispin. 'Course, she would've been Rachel Pepper then.'

Callisto starts as if a wasp has stung him. His eyes take on a regretful expression. 'Rachel!' he whispers.

'You and her was friends, wasn't you, sir?'

'Yes,' says Callisto. 'She was my assistant for almost two years, and we grew to be ... friends, but we fell out, I'm afraid. I'm not the kind of man that it's easy to be friends with.' He gazes searchingly at Crispin, detects the mother's features in the son's, and understands why he liked the lad at first sight. 'So, you're Rachel's boy,' he says.

'That I am, sir!'

'Tell me your story, Crispin Rattle,' says Callisto, 'and mind you make it quick.'

Crispin squares his shoulders and says in

a rush, 'Ma and Pa died two days before the postman brung this letter. They got buried by the parish and next day the landlord turned me out. I didn't have nowhere to go, so I thought I might as well come and see you, sir.'

Callisto looks at the sheet of paper again and purses his lips. 'Who would want to send your mother a coded message, I wonder?'

'So do I, sir!' says Crispin.

Callisto thinks back and back. He remembers Rachel with her hair loose, staring out through a rainy window; dressed in her stage costume, smiling a wide, false smile. He hears her voice scolding him, pleading with him. And then he recalls a conversation they once had in York railway station, when they were on tour together. 'Your mother had two older brothers, didn't she?' he says. 'Malachi and Jasper. Why didn't you go to them?'

Crispin frowns so deeply that his entire face puckers. 'Ma never said nothing to me about no brothers, sir,' he says.

Callisto is not surprised to hear this. The Rachel he knew was wild, and had run away from home to join a circus, or a theatre, or a pirate ship – anything so long as it was not what her parents wanted for her. Her past was over, she often said, and she wanted nothing more to do with it.

'D'you think the letter might be important, sir?' says Crispin.

'Almost certainly,' Callisto says. 'Otherwise whoever sent it wouldn't have gone to the trouble of encoding it.'

Crispin leans forward in the chair. 'Can you make sense of it for me, sir?'

'Perhaps,' says Callisto, 'but it may take me some time. Leave it with me and I'll see what I can do. Where can I contact you?'

'Contact me, sir?'

'Where are you lodging?'

Crispin cannot look Callisto in the face, so he looks at the floor instead. 'Nowhere, sir,' he mumbles. 'Slept on a bench in a park last night.'

Aril puts her hand on Callisto's arm and gently squeezes. They exchange a glance that says much.

Callisto adopts a brisk tone. 'I've a business proposition to put to you, Crispin Rattle. I live in Scarlatti Mews – d'you know where that is?'

'No, sir,' admits Crispin.

'No matter,' says Callisto. 'If you can bear to wait here until after this evening's show, Aril and I will accompany you there. I offer you free board and lodging until I've decoded the letter, or it becomes obvious that I'm unable to decode it. If the letter should happen to put you in possession of a handsome fortune, I shall expect to receive a fee to be agreed upon at a later date. What do you say?'

Crispin does not say much. He bursts into tears and snivels out a long sentence in which the only recognizable words are 'kindness' and 'thankful'.

CHAPTER FIVE
IN LONDON

The 4.45 p.m. train from Wolveston pulls into London Station right on time. A single passenger alights on Platform One. He is Jasper Pepper.

There can be no denying that Jasper is a distinguished-looking man. His nose is aquiline, his eyes are blue, his jaw is firm, and over each ear a wing of prematurely white hair sweeps through the black. He is dressed in a double-breasted overcoat, plaid trousers, patent-leather capped boots and a curly-brimmed bowler hat. This outfit is the very height of fashion – or 'quite the go', as they would say in Wolveston – but it is unlikely that anyone in a dull backwater like London knows enough about fashion to appreciate Jasper's good taste. Any Londoner who catches sight of him will gain the impression that here is a sober and sensible man, trustworthy, honest and open-handed. Nothing, alas, could be further from the truth.

Once he leaves the station, Jasper turns his collar up against the cold and casts about for a cab. He spies one loitering beneath a gas lamp. The cab appears as dilapidated as the horse that is harnessed to it and the driver who holds the reins.

Jasper raises his arm and calls out, 'Hello, cabman! Over here, if you please.'

But it evidently does not please the cabman, for he stays just where he is.

Jasper walks to the cab and glares up at the driver. 'Are you deaf, man?' he demands.

'Don't think so,' says the cabman.

'Then why didn't you come when I called you?'

The cabman shrugs. 'Didn't much feel like it, did I?'

Anger blazes in Jasper's eyes. 'I'll require you to mind your manners, fellow!'

'If you don't like my manners, you can take another cab,' says the cabman. 'It's all the same to me, mate.'

Jasper glances at the empty street. 'But there isn't another cab!' he exclaims.

'No, and there won't be another, not tonight anyroad,' says the cabman. 'If you wants driving anywhere, you'll have to put up with me, won't you?'

Jasper fumes and taps his foot petulantly. He opens the door of the cab and barks, 'Take me to the Asmodeus Arms!'

After a nonchalant pause, the cabman says, 'Walk on, boy!' and the horse lurches forward.

Jasper has not been idle since the night he committed the corpse of his brother to the watery bosom of the Bast. He has called in many favours and brought certain pressures to bear. Electoral rolls and police records have been opened to him, and he has been granted access to sources of information not readily available to members of the general public. Jasper Pepper is a surprisingly influential man, and the power he exercises over those who share his unconventional beliefs is considerable.

The Asmodeus Arms is a tavern, close to the River Thames, in fact so close that the river is an occasional occupant. It is a rickety, rackety building whose walls and roofs lean in such violently different directions that the tavern does not stand so much as slouch. On the sign hanging outside is painted the face of Asmodeus, the ancient Persian demon of rage and infidelity. The features manage to be both human and leonine, and the mouth is bared in a snarl that reveals fearsomely long sharp teeth.

As Jasper steps out of the cab he catches sight of the sign and smiles admiringly, for he considers the likeness to be reasonably accurate. He pays off the saucy cabman and enters the tavern.

The interior is dingy and dank. The air is heavy with the mixed odours of stale tobacco smoke, rum and skulduggery. Besides Jasper there are only two customers: an old man seated in a corner, who stares at nothing, and a drunken sailor sprawled face-down on a table.

Behind the bar of the tavern stands a plump man with a florid complexion and excessive side whiskers which give him the look of an overfed sheep. He sees Jasper, smells money and gives the bar a wipe with a damp cloth that is so filthy, it leaves the wooden surface dirtier than it was before. 'Good evening, sir!' the man says. 'What's your pleasure?'

If Jasper were to be perfectly honest, the answer to this question would occupy several minutes, but he contents himself with, 'Information. Are you Lucan Treddle?'

The man behind the bar frowns and thinks of detectives, debt-collectors and insurance salesmen. 'Who wants to know?' he says.

'That is none of your concern,' Jasper tells him. 'I'm making enquiries about some relatives of mine, the Rattle family. Until quite recently, you were their landlord, were you not?'

'What if I was?'

Jasper's experience of conversations such as this advises that the moment is ripe to offer an incentive. He places a gold coin on the bar. 'Tell me what I want to know and I'll provide companions for that,' he says.

Lucan Treddle is still suspicious, but gold is gold and he swiftly pockets the coin. 'Yeah, I let out one of my properties to the Rattles,' he says. 'Tragic how that young boy got orphaned. Fair broke my heart to think of how he was left all alone in the world with no one to look after him.'

'What happened to him?' asked Jasper.

'Couldn't pay the rent, could he?' Lucan replies. 'Had to put him out, didn't I? He scarpered off quick-like. Property's empty now, costing me money. I don't suppose that you—?'

'No,' interrupts Jasper. 'I don't suppose either. Did the boy leave a forwarding address?'

Lucan shakes his head.

'Did he give you any indication of where he might be bound?' says Jasper.

'We weren't exactly what you'd call intimately acquainted,' Lucan confesses. 'He could be dead in a ditch for all I know. Didn't take much with him, wherever he went. I cleared two tea chests of papers and knick-knacks out the place.'

Jasper inhales sharply. 'And what became of those tea chests?'

'Down in my cellar,' says Lucan. 'I been meaning to go through 'em, see if there's anything of value that needs keeping safe in case the boy comes back.'

Jasper produces another gold coin and twirls it between the fingers of his right hand. The coin winks rhythmically in the light from the lamp above the bar.

'Show me,' Jasper says.

Lucan Treddle wants to tell Jasper to sling his hook and go to blazes, but he finds himself quite unable to. For reasons that he cannot fathom, he is suddenly intensely fond of this gentlemanly stranger from nowhere. 'Certainly, sir!' he coos. 'If you'd care to step this way?'

Because he is a methodical man, it takes Jasper the best part of two hours to work through the tea chests. His surroundings are not pleasant. The cellar walls weep damp and are coated with a glistening white crust. The corners are hung with cobwebs as thick as leather.

Jasper unpacks old notices, candle-ends, shopping lists, cracked china, cheap plaster figures, but doesn't find what he is looking for. He gnaws the inner surface of his bottom lip. Only one item in the chests is in the least remarkable, and he spreads it out over a barrel of porter and brings his stub of candle closer.

It is a yellowing poster, advertising an evening of magic and mystery at the Standard Theatre, Cornwall Street, Wolveston. Jasper knows that the poster is an old one, for the Standard Theatre burned down years since. Top of the bill is 'The Great Wizard of the North, Professor Anderson', and the poster is decorated with drawings of the professor pouring wine from a small bottle into many glasses, producing a shower of bank notes from a top hat and waving a wand at a small flock of birds. The rest of the poster announces, 'The Mesmeric Couch', 'The

Great Gun Trick' and the like. At the very bottom, inside a small box, is printed, 'Tonight only, the Inimitable Callisto and his lovely assistant Rachel'.

Jasper muses. Rachel was his sister's name, it is true, but could she ever have been described as 'lovely'? He casts his mind back. His memories of his sister are not affectionate, but he recalls her feistiness, her stubborn temper and her defiance. A life in the theatre as a conjuror's assistant may have been a possible career for his estranged sibling. It cannot have been a successful career though, or she would not have fetched up in London.

Jasper stares at the poster, certain that he has discovered a vital clue, but a vital clue to what? He sighs, knowing that he has come to the limits of what human knowledge can offer him. Further investigation will involve robes, a pentagram, and a considerable quantity of blood.

Chapter Six
Scarlatti Mews

When Callisto puts on his evening performance at the Egyptian Hall, a stage-struck Crispin Rattle watches from the wings. Nothing that he has witnessed on the streets of London has prepared him for this spectacle, and it leaves him dazzled and dumbfounded. In his eyes, Callisto is a sort of god and Aril is an angel of such loveliness that Crispin is almost in awe of her. When they come off stage, the boy does not know whether to clap, cheer or fall to his knees and offer them a prayer. In the end, he offers them the longest word he knows and declares, 'That was prodigious!'

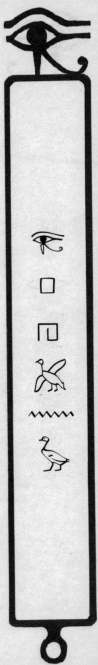

With little more ado, Callisto and Aril change out of their costumes and leave the Egyptian Hall via the stage door, taking Crispin with them. A knot of people has gathered, clamouring to shake Callisto's hand, or slap him on the back, or collect his autograph. After Callisto has fulfilled his obligations to his public, Aril and Crispin follow him into the crowds that bustle along Broadway. The thoroughfare twinkles and glitters with so many lights that for a moment Crispin thinks that all the stars must have fallen down from the night sky.

At length, they reach Broadway Station and descend, via Cobbleday's ingenious Steam Staircase, to a platform on the Intrapolitan Line of the Wolveston Subterranean Railway. Crispin finds that travelling beneath the earth by train is also prodigious; indeed, the whole day has been the most prodigious of his life. After five stops the train reaches Bywater, and

Callisto, Aril and Crispin get off. From Bywater Station it is a short stroll to Scarlatti Mews.

Scarlatti Mews, as pretty a part of Wolveston as may be found, was constructed in a more tranquil, more modest age. Its buildings – too small for houses and too large for cottages – stand shoulder to shoulder like steadfast comrades, around a cobbled square. There are pantiled roofs, trim front gardens and if the doors do not actually have roses twining round them, most have vegetation of one kind or another. After the hubbub of the city streets, the quietness of Scarlatti Mews is as welcome as a cool drink on a broiling day.

'Cor!' Crispin exclaims. 'This is just like London – but cleaner.'

Callisto and Aril lead the way through the gate of Number 17 and up the garden path. Callisto holds a key at the ready, but before he can insert it into any lock, the front door swings open and there is Mrs Moncrief, lit by the light of the paraffin-oil lamp that she holds in her left hand.

Callisto is uncertain of exactly how old his housekeeper is and he is too much of a gentleman to enquire, but clearly the first flush of youth is well behind her. Mrs Moncrief is tall and thin, grey of hair, pale of eye and long of nose. Constantly in mourning for the late Mr Moncrief, she always dresses in black.

The smile that she turns on Callisto is like the beam of a lighthouse. 'Good evening, Mr Callisto!' she proclaims in a loud, piercing voice.

'Evening, Mrs M,' says Callisto.

The beam brightens as Mrs Moncrief regards Aril, 'And a good evening to you, Miss Aril!'

'Good evening, Mrs Moncrief.'

But when Mrs Moncrief turns to Crispin, her beam is extinguished. Her eyes bulge and roll, and her free hand flies to her bony bosom. 'Who is this that you have brought with you, Mr Callisto?' she demands. 'Is it some spirit conjured from the vasty deep?'

Callisto cocks his head to one side and says, 'Beg pardon, Mrs M?'

'Who is this boy? What is he doing here?'

Crispin answers for himself. 'Please, ma'am, I'm Crispin Rattle and I'm an orphan.'

Mrs Moncrief's hand flies from her bosom to her forehead. 'An orphan?' she shrieks. 'I understand all too well, for if Providence had blessed my dear dead husband and myself with a child, that child would be a half-orphan today. Embrace me, Crispin Rattle!'

'Embrace you, ma'am?' says Crispin, taken aback.

'Nothing less will do!' cries Mrs Moncrief, and she hugs the boy awkwardly, taking care not to set him on fire with the lamp.

The tableau thus presented is touching, but bizarre.

Callisto clears his throat. 'Mrs Moncrief, might I trouble you to set an extra place at the supper table?'

Mrs Moncrief releases Crispin from her grip. 'That will be no trouble, Mr Callisto,' she says. 'No trouble whatsoever!' and she flounces down the hallway.

Crispin whispers to Aril from the side of his mouth, 'Does she often take on like that?'

'All the time,' Aril whispers back. 'She wanted to be an actress when she was young, but she wasn't considered to be good enough. She treats her life as a drama to make up for it.'

Containing, as it does, a magician, an angel and a madwoman, Crispin concludes that life in Callisto's household is unlikely to be dull.

* * *

Three places have been laid on the tiny table in the tiny dining room. Though the table is small, it has been spread with a bewildering array of cold meats, pies, pickles, fruit, cake, bread, water, wine and ale. Callisto carves, serves and pours, and Crispin can hardly believe the quantity of food that is piled on his plate. He is more used to the heel of a loaf, spread with dripping or dipped in gravy. In a wonderstruck voice he says, 'This ain't a supper – it's a feast!'

It is a feast that he is unable to enjoy for long, however. The comfort of a full belly and the cosiness of his surroundings soon overcome him with dark waves of sleep, and he slumbers where he sits.

Callisto gently gathers Crispin up and carries him into the back parlour, where Mrs Moncrief has erected a collapsible bed, once part of an elaborate stage illusion, now reduced to the menial trick of providing accommodation for an unexpected guest. Callisto draws a blanket over the sleeping boy and steps out into the hall, where he meets Mrs Moncrief. 'I apologize for the lack of notice, Mrs M,' he says. 'The lad turned up in my dressing room just like that. He came from London and I think he must have walked most of the way. I fear that he's somewhat grubby.'

'Nothing that hot water and soap won't remedy,' says Mrs Moncrief. 'He'll scrub up as shiny as a sixpence.' Her eyes narrow. 'I hope this isn't going to be the start of one of your escapades, Mr Callisto.'

'I'm not planning any escapades, Mrs M,' Callisto assures her. 'Crispin is simply an unfortunate soul in need of a helping hand.'

'That's what you said about the flower-girl from Bude,' Mrs Moncrief says accusingly.

'Now, now, Mrs M! Didn't we agree not

to mention her again?' says Callisto. 'I give you my most solemn promise – no more escapades!'

Mrs Moncrief sniffs. She knows Callisto's solemn promises of old.

Callisto returns to the supper table, takes a glass of wine and once more examines Crispin's mysterious letter. 'It doesn't appear to be Caesar's cipher,' he mutters. 'A pound to a pinch of snuff it's Vigenère's.'

Aril puts down her knife and fork. 'What are you burbling about?' she says. 'And who is Vigenère?'

'He was a French diplomat in the sixteenth century,' Callisto informs her. 'He devised a revolutionary new code. You take a square and divide it into smaller squares with twenty-six vertical lines and twenty-six horizontal lines. Then you write out the letters of the alphabet—'

The description of the process is long

and rather tedious, and Aril doesn't pay close attention to it.

'So, as you can appreciate, having the key phrase is vital,' Callisto says in conclusion. 'Without it, the code can't be cracked. Unfortunately in this case, only two people knew the key phrase. One is dead and we have no idea who the other one is ... and I've bored you to tears, haven't I?'

'No, to sleep,' says Aril, with a yawn. 'I must go to bed.' She rises from her chair, rests a hand on Callisto's shoulder and kisses his cheek. 'Are you being kind to Crispin for his mother's sake?'

'And my own sake,' says Callisto. 'I didn't do right by her. This is a chance for me to make amends.'

Aril crosses the room and pauses in the doorway. 'Crispin hasn't told us everything, you know,' she says.

'Has he not?' says Callisto.

'He's keeping something from us,

something that he's afraid of,' Aril says. 'He's carrying a darkness with him.'

'Then we will lighten that darkness at the earliest available opportunity,' Callisto says.

Aril leaves and Mrs Moncrief enters to clear away the supper things. She presents Callisto with the latest edition of the *Evening Hermes*, which Callisto is in the habit of browsing through before retiring. It is Wolveston's most sensational news-paper – if 'newspaper' is the correct term to apply to a publication that contains so much sensation and so little news. Most of the front page is taken up by a scandal involving a Member of Parliament and a female trapeze artiste. Page two concerns itself with the tale of a family whose lives were saved by a St Bernard dog during a blizzard in the Grampian Mountains. But tucked away at the foot of page three is a small item that causes Callisto to sit bolt upright.

CORPSE IN RIVER NAMED

Devon Court detectives announced this morning that the body of a man suffering from a gunshot wound, discovered in the River Bast near Toolham a fortnight ago, may be that of Malachi Pepper (aged 50), resident of 27 Bearwood Street. Mr Pepper's employer, Mr Luigi Febbo of Febbo's Antique Curios, Lollard Lane, reported him as missing more than a month since. Those who have any information regarding the state of Mr Pepper's mind at the time of his disappearance are urged to contact Woveston Civic Constabulary Headquarters without delay. Mr Febbo has offered a generous reward to anyone who can provide evidence that will lead to a satisfactory explanation of Mr Pepper's death.

Malachi Pepper! thinks Callisto. Brother of Jasper and Rachel Pepper. Malachi Pepper, whose nephew lies asleep in my parlour . . .

Callisto smiles, and under his breath murmurs, 'Sorry, Mrs M!' for another escapade is about to begin.

CHAPTER SEVEN
A RENDEZVOUS IN TAFFIT
SQUARE

Upon his return to Wolveston, Jasper Pepper proceeds by cab to his house in Monksbane Close and arrives shortly before midnight. Monksbane Close is located in one of the most exclusive districts of the capital and its inhabitants are either titled, extremely wealthy, or both. Remarkably, Jasper is neither. The riches he draws on are not of this world, and in place of abundant property, he possesses abundant power. There are some peculiar goings-on at Jasper's house, but if any other residents of the close notice them, they pass no comment, as to show an

interest in the affairs of a neighbour would be considered offensively vulgar.

At midnight Jasper goes down into his cellar and there performs a nameless and unspeakable rite which leaves him tired and light-headed, with a bandage on his left arm and an appointment that must be kept. The light-headedness and the bandage are due to Jasper's having shed almost a pint of his own blood. He climbs the cellar stairs to the kitchen, where he drinks a large mug of sweet, milky tea before catching a few hours' sleep on a sofa.

Although there are no visible servants in the house, when Jasper wakes at seven o'clock the following morning, more tea awaits him, steaming in a china cup and saucer, and when he goes up to the bathroom, a hot bath has been drawn and his shaving kit is neatly laid out on a white towel. As he soaps his face, Jasper prepares himself for the ordeal that lies ahead. He will need to keep his wits about him. If he is too direct, he will be avoided; if he is not direct enough, he will be misled. Any break in his concentration, however momentary, will have permanent consequences. He has learned that it always pays to be wary in the company of a demon, even a demon that he has raised himself.

At precisely ten a.m. Jasper enters Taffit Square, where the well-to-do congregate to see and be seen. The square is laid out in something of the style of an Italian piazza. The buildings that surround it are riddled with arcades of shops, the most illustrious of which are couturiers, furriers and jewellers. Pavement cafés are dotted around the square. It is a spot that attracts many tourists, for at its centre, standing on a plinth in the midst of a pool fed by fountains, is the memorial statue of Sir Daniel Taffit. Taffit was the engineering genius who designed and built the Great Eastern Canal that links Wolveston to the great Norfolk ports. This line of communication is so vital to the economic welfare of the nation that troops are garrisoned along its length to protect it. Starting the canal cost Taffit his reputation; completing it cost him his fortune and his life. Scorned and ridiculed while he was alive, Taffit was awarded a posthumous knighthood within hours of his death and the monument, funded by public subscription, followed a year later.

Jasper walks at a leisurely pace and his impassively calm expression betrays no hint of the storm of apprehension raging within him. Encountering demons by daylight is a dangerous business, but Jasper was given no choice in the matter, and he understands that to win rich returns he must wager high stakes. As he passes the Café Rio, Jasper detects the fragrance of coffee on the air, and a quite different smell, a pungency that vanishes almost as soon as he is aware of it.

'Why, Jasper Pepper!' says a voice. 'Fancy meeting you here!'

Jasper turns.

The demon has taken the form of a young woman who is, appropriately enough, devilishly pretty. She is dressed in striped satin and lace, and a delicious concoction of a hat is perched upon her head. Her eyes are as blue as tropical lagoons, her button nose is as cute as a basket of kittens and her mouth is the tender bud of some exotic flower. The deep chestnut-brown locks of her hair have been carefully arranged to conceal the tips of her ears, and her hands are encased in grey leather gloves. She is seated at a table and she gestures to an empty chair. 'Won't you join me?'

Jasper removes his hat and sits. 'Thank you, Bazimaal.'

The young woman snorts. 'Really,

Jasper!' she scolds. 'You should know better than to speak my name in public. The knowing of names is the beginning of enthralment, and I have no intention of being in thrall to any man, especially you.' She looks around. 'It's been so long that I'd completely forgotten how solid all this is, and how demanding a body can be. All those urgent drives and appetites – how do you bear them?'

'Patiently,' says Jasper.

A waiter wearing a blue apron appears meaningfully beside the table.

'Will you take something?' Jasper asks the young woman.

She flutters her eyelashes at the waiter. 'Perhaps a small glass of brandy?'

'Certainly, miss,' says the waiter. 'French or Welsh?'

'Oh, Welsh!' she chimes, tipping the waiter a wink. 'I feel in the mood for something Celtic.'

'And I'll have a café noir,' says Jasper. He

waits until the waiter is out of earshot before he continues, 'Shall we to business?'

'And what business would that be, Jasper?'

'You know very well!' Jasper replies curtly.

The young woman shrugs. 'One either knows something or one does not. I don't see that degrees of quality of knowing come into it. Quantity, however, is a different matter. How much of what I know would you like to know?'

This demon has come equipped with tricks and booby-traps, but Jasper knows it of old and will not allow himself to be ensnared. 'I would like to know a limited amount about one thing in particular,' he says.

'Oh, bravo, clever Jasper!' purrs the young woman. 'And what precisely would you like to know about this particular thing?'

'Its location,' Jasper says.

They are interrupted by the waiter delivering their order. Jasper spoons sugar into his coffee.

The young woman touches the stem of her brandy glass and the liquor inside evaporates in a puff of pale flame. 'Exquisite!' she sighs. 'Now, as to location – are you listening carefully?'

'You have my undivided attention,' Jasper says.

'It's not on the earth, or on the water, or under the water,' says the young woman. 'It's hidden in plain view, in a place where many go but none stays.'

Jasper expects the young woman to continue. When she does not, he demands, 'Is that all?'

'That is everything.'

'But what am I supposed to make of it?'

'Whatever you wish.' The young woman reaches across the table and touches Jasper's sleeve. 'Be warned, Jasper Pepper. If the price of your heart's desire is your

74

heart itself, what good will come of it? Are you truly certain that you want what you want? What if it should be less than you imagined? What if it's not there at all?'

'Why don't you tell me what I wish to know, and then leave me alone to drink my coffee in peace?' Jasper says petulantly.

The young woman frowns, and withdraws her hand. 'You're so ungracious, Jasper,' she says. 'What you take, you take with a mean spirit. You'll never be happy, or even content.'

'Contentment is for the small-minded and happiness is best left to children and to fools,' says Jasper. 'It's ambition that drives me.'

'Ambition?' the young woman says with a mocking laugh. 'I'd rather say that you are driven by hatred of humanity, Jasper. Once you have what you want, you will use it to change this world out of all recognition. How many will die on your account?'

Jasper's eyes are dreamy. 'Millions, hopefully!' he says.

The young woman shakes her head in sorrow. 'Just think of all the assistance you've forced me to give you to further your wicked ends!'

'You have not assisted me in the slightest,' Jasper rejoins. 'You have hindered and thwarted me at every turn, made empty promises, duped me, hoodwinked me and made me your fool.'

'And I have also lied to you,' the young woman reminds him. 'I have lied about everything . . . except the Black Sphinx. Its power will render you invincible and irresistible.'

Jasper smiles fondly. 'Among the first things I shall do when the sphinx is mine is to give you all that you deserve, dear Bazimaal,' he vows.

The young woman's face blanches. 'Don't go any further with this, Jasper!' she pleads. 'Walk away from it now, before it's too late.'

'It has always been too late for me,' says Jasper.

He is talking to an empty glass and an empty chair; the young woman has gone.

Jasper thinks. *Not on the earth, or on the water, or in the water.* Where then – in the air? On a mountain? Aboard a hot-air balloon? Or perhaps the object is lodged on the upper floor of some tall building, of which Wolveston has many. Which one, which one?

Ignored and untasted, Jasper's coffee gradually goes cold.

CHAPTER EIGHT
AT THE LODGING HOUSE

When Crispin Rattle sits down to breakfast in Scarlatti Mews on Sunday morning, he is hardly recognizable. The travel-stained ragamuffin has gone. Under the influences of hot water, soap and a flannel the lad has come up just this side of cherubic, though his costume still leaves something to be desired. His old clothes being deemed suitable only for burning, Crispin is wearing some of Callisto's cast-offs, which are too large and fit only where they touch. Crispin is in need of new boots, but will have to wait for them until the shops open on Monday. For the time being, he must make do with

a pair of curly-toed Turkish slippers. Crispin finds these splendid, but wonders how the Turks manage with such peculiarly shaped feet. If their toes twist up like that, trimming the nails must be murder! he thinks.

Breakfast is every bit as sumptuous as supper was, and Crispin does it justice. As the meal winds down towards the toast-and-marmalade stage, Callisto says, 'I'm afraid I have some bad news for you, Crispin.'

'You ain't changed your mind about me staying here, have you?' says Crispin, dismayed.

'No,' says Callisto. 'The news concerns your uncle, Malachi Pepper. He has been murdered.'

'Sorry to hear it, Mr Callisto,' chirps Crispin, though truth to tell he is not sorry in the least. He cannot feel any grief for a man he never knew.

'Some aspects of your uncle's case

intrigue me, and I mean to conduct my own investigation,' Callisto says. 'I'll make a start this morning by visiting Malachi Pepper's lodgings in Bearwood Street.'

'And I'll come with you!' declares Crispin, and when he sees the doubtful look on Callisto's face, he adds, 'He was *my* uncle, after all.'

Callisto concedes Crispin's point with a nod.

'I'll come along as well,' says Aril.

Callisto turns to her. 'Are you quite sure that's wise?' he asks. 'You have exercises to perform, don't you? Don't forget, it isn't long until the full moon.'

Crispin does not have the least idea what the moon has to do with anything, but Aril apparently does. 'All right,' she says, but the flash of annoyance in her eyes and the pout on her lips are strongly suggestive of resentment.

After breakfast Callisto goes upstairs. When he reappears some half an hour later, he has transformed himself. He sports a splendid moustache and his waistcoat is stretched a shade too tightly across his padded belly. He wears a blue suit and a black bowler hat, and carries a cheap document-case made of cardboard masquerading as leather.

'Swipe me!' Crispin cries. 'Why the disguise, Mr Callisto? You look like a clerk.'

'That's my intention,' says Callisto. 'I'm well known from the stage, and people don't always take magicians seriously. There are times when it is necessary for me to assume another identity.'

'Shall I put on a disguise too?' Crispin says.

Callisto considers Crispin's ill-fitting clothes and curly-toed footwear. 'I think you'll do just as you are, Crispin,' he says.

Callisto and Crispin walk smartly down Bearwood Street. Rubbish festers in the gutters and there are unsavoury stains on the pavement. The houses look neglected and run-down. Slates are missing from roofs; paintwork peels and stonework crumbles. Such curtains as hang in the dingy windows are yellowed and tattered.

Bearwood Street stands at the very edge of northwest Wolveston and the very limit of law and order. Those who travel beyond will find themselves in the city's most notorious district, the human sink that is known as 'The Scarp'. All classes of criminals haunt it, all life within it is low and cheap. Law-abiding citizens do not venture into the Scarp unless they are armed with revolvers; respectable citizens do not go there at all. The police are rare visitors, and the sight of a police uniform on the streets of the Scarp would be enough to incite a riot. It is a place which makes and abides by its own rules.

Callisto and Crispin stop at Number 27 and Callisto knocks at the door.

The response is slow, but at last a window on the first floor screeches open and a head and shoulders are thrust out. The head and shoulders belong to Mrs Gavel, to whom the property likewise belongs. She is a round woman, with grey hair scraped back into a bun, a face like a pug dog's and a temper to match. 'What you want?' she demands brusquely.

Callisto doffs his cap. 'Pardon the intrusion, madam, but I'm enquiring about a Mr Malachi Pepper. I believe he used to live here.'

Mrs Gavel's face darkens. 'Yes, he was a tenant of mine – worst luck! You know he's dead?'

Callisto nods.

'Well I wish he was alive, so I could kill him!' Mrs Gavel snaps. 'The aggravation that man's caused me.'

'How did Mr Pepper seem when you saw him last?' asks Callisto.

'He seemed like a man who owed me a week's rent and sagged off without paying it,' Mrs Gavel replies.

Callisto pats his jacket pocket and coins clink. 'I may be able to assist you regarding that unpaid bill.'

The words have scarcely left his mouth before bolts are being drawn and the door opens just wide enough for one of Mrs Gavel's eyeballs to glare out. 'Blokes don't go round paying other blokes' rents unless there's something in it for 'em,' Mrs Gavel says. 'What's your game?'

'I'm an agent for an insurance company – Mousewhite and Mousewhite. Perhaps you've heard of us.'

'If I did, I forgot about it straight off,' Mrs Gavel mutters. 'Who's this you've got with you?'

'My errand boy, Toby,' says Callisto. 'He follows me like a shadow.'

Crispin draws back his shoulders and tries his best to look shadow-like.

'Is he all right in the head?' Mrs Gavel demands.

'Why yes,' Callisto assures her.

'Then why's he wearing them shoes?'

Callisto leans forward and says in an undertone, 'It's not his fault. He's from London.'

'Ah, say no more!' says Mrs Gavel. 'Now, what d'you want from me?'

'Mr Pepper took out a life insurance policy with us a few weeks before he died,' says Callisto. 'If his death is proved to be an accident or foul play, Mousewhite and Mousewhite will be obliged to honour the terms of that policy—'

Mrs Gavel is ahead of him. 'But if he topped himself, you won't have to pay up.'

'Succinctly put, madam,' says Callisto. He reaches into his pocket, withdraws a gold coin and offers it to Mrs Gavel.

'I ain't got no change,' she says.

'I wouldn't require any, if you were to grant me a favour,' says Callisto.

'What favour's that then?'

'Let me inspect Mr Pepper's lodgings. It won't take long, and I'll be sure to leave things as I find them.'

Mrs Gavel laughs, though it sounds more like the wheezing and gurgling of a kettle on the point of boiling. 'Leave things as you find 'em?' she chortles. 'That's a good'un and no mistake!' She takes the coin and ushers Callisto into the house. 'It's upstairs, first door on the left.'

Callisto and Crispin climb the staircase. Callisto opens the door and a draught sends white feathers swirling through the air like a flurry of snow. The feathers come from two slashed pillows. The room has been ransacked pretty much as thoroughly as a room *can* be ransacked. Furniture has been disassembled, the mattress on the broken bed has been filleted and in places floorboards have been taken up.

'Strewth!' gasps Crispin.

Mrs Gavel, who is standing behind him, says, 'Been done proper, ain't it?'

'When did this happen?' says Callisto.

'Three days after Mr Pepper went missing.'

'Have you informed the police?'

'Why waste my breath? They won't do nothing,' Mrs Gavel says. 'Whoever done this knew what they were about. I didn't see 'em or hear 'em.' She jerks her head in the direction of the Scarp. 'If anything's been took, it's probably over there.'

'Who would take such pains over searching a man's room?' Callisto says, thinking aloud.

Crispin, summing it up neatly, says, 'Someone who was looking for something.'

CHAPTER NINE
AN UNEXPECTED VISITOR

Lollard Lane forms part of the South Bank, one of Wolveston's oldest districts. From the northern end of the lane there is a fine view across the Bast to the Lord Protector's Palace with its towers and turrets, from one of which flies the flag of Greater Britain, a silver dragon passant on a field of azure. The sun reflects from the myriad windows of the palace, making the building appear as if it has been constructed of light.

Lollard Lane is a winding procession of booksellers, fine art and antique dealers, clock makers, carpenters and furniture restorers. Since it is Sunday the shops are closed, but in the back room of his premises Luigi Febbo, until lately the employer of Malachi Pepper, is at work. In the early hours of the morning a package was delivered to him and he is engaged in examining its contents.

Luigi has silver hair, expressive brown eyes, an olive complexion, a dimpled chin, and is something of a ladies' man, which accounts for his having fought several duels. The sign above his shop characterizes him as a 'dealer' in antiquities, but this is only half the story, for Luigi is also a *supplier* of antiquities, and he is none too fussy about where he obtains his supplies. For instance, the gold and lapis lazuli necklace he is currently squinting at through the lens of a magnifying glass was, until recently, in a private collection in Vienna. The exact details of how the necklace comes to be in Wolveston and into whose hands it will finally be delivered are matters that Luigi would be reluctant to reveal, but they are matters which will turn him a handsome profit.

While Luigi Febbo is thus occupied, unbeknownst to him a large black coach with frosted-glass windows is being drawn down Lollard Lane by a pair of dapple-grey Clydesdale horses. At the front of the coach sits a driver and beside him sits a guard, who holds a carbine in the crook of his left arm. Standing at the back of the coach are two footmen, liveried in pale green satin, with powdered periwigs on their heads. The footman on the right has a scar on his cheek; the footman on the left has a broken nose.

The coachman demonstrates considerable skill in negotiating the narrow way, and at last he draws up outside Febbo's Antique Curios. The footmen jump down and stride over to the door of the shop. The scarred man pulls a short, broad-bladed crowbar from inside his jacket and with a deft wrench separates the door from its lock. The footmen step inside, just in time to see Luigi Febbo emerge from the back room. Luigi is holding a pistol but its hammer is uncocked, unlike the hammer of the Navy Colt that the broken-nosed footman is aiming at him. The footman says quietly, 'Give it up!' and Luigi drops his gun to the floor. The scar-faced footman crosses the shop, seizes Luigi by the back of his collar and the seat of his trousers and frog-marches him to the doorway.

The guard, who has climbed down from his place, reaches over to open the door of the coach. A woman steps out onto the pavement. She is wearing a black silk dress that froths with black lace, a pair of white gloves and a black hat topped with a yellow silk rose. The woman is between thirty and forty years of age, her figure is plump and fulsome, her hair is dark, her eyes are jade green and her features are arresting. Many hearts have been broken on her account; many windows and many faces have also been broken. She has dined with both the highest and the lowest in the land and is on intimate terms with several cabinet ministers and foreign ambassadors. When President Garbridge of the Federal Union of America paid a state visit to Wolveston, he was a guest in one of the woman's many houses. Her name is Squalida MacHeath and she is Wolveston's undisputed, if uncrowned, Queen of Crime.

Luigi Febbo knows who she is, and his knowledge manifests itself in the trembling of his limbs, the pallor of his face and the beads of sweat that stand out on his brow.

Squalida gazes at the shivering dealer in antiquities and says, in a gently exasperated tone, 'Oh, Luigi, what am I to do with you? You've been a bad boy, haven't you? A very bad boy indeed.'

Since Luigi is temporarily at a loss as to exactly what he has done to earn Squalida MacHeath's disapproval, he begins with a general-purpose, one-size-fits-all grovel. 'Miss MacHeath, I swear I did not know!' he grizzles. 'As God is my witness!'

'But God isn't your witness, Luigi,' Squalida points out. 'The sole witnesses present are my men, and they'll see only what I tell them to see.'

Luigi's mind fumbles about like a man searching for his slippers in a darkened bedroom. 'Forgive me, please!' he begs. 'I will never, never do it again!'

'That's for certain,' says Squalida, 'but I'm far more interested in why you did it in the first place. You sauntered into the Scarp, bold as kiss-my-elbow, and hired Johnny Feltch and Tom Harcourt – two of my top housebreakers – to do a job for you. And did you seek my permission, or offer me a share of the take? You did not!' Squalida MacHeath makes a tutting sound. 'If there's one thing I can't abide, it's bad manners, Luigi. Why, I wouldn't have known anything about the break-in if Johnny and Tom hadn't ratted on each other.'

'What can I say, Miss MacHeath?' wails Luigi. 'I could not share the take with you because there *was* no take. Johnny Feltch and Tom Harcourt did not find what I wanted.'

Squalida's eyes twinkle. 'Ah, now we're coming to it!' she says. 'I wish to learn more about what it is you wanted. You hired Johnny and Tom to search for a statuette in a house in Bearwood Street, and you paid them twice the going rate for a burglary. That's a deal of money to lay out for an ornament.'

'It was my mother's!' blusters Luigi. 'It is of sentimental value.'

Squalida throws back her head and laughs. 'Why, Luigi, you haven't got a sentimental bone in your body! Tell me about the statuette.'

Luigi's eyes dart this way and that, as if looking for an escape from his skull. 'I cannot!' he croaks. 'I would put my immortal soul in danger. It is more than my life is worth.'

Squalida motions to the broken-nosed footman, who presses the muzzle of his revolver against the back of Luigi's head.

'Taking one thing with another, Luigi, your life doesn't appear to be worth that much at the moment, does it?' says Squalida.

Luigi whimpers, then says reluctantly, 'Six months ago, a man by the name of Jasper Pepper approached me to procure an item for him, an ancient Egyptian statuette of a black sphinx that he had seen in a museum in St Petersburg. This I arranged for him and the sphinx was duly delivered to me, but before I could hand it over to Pepper, it was stolen by my bookkeeper.'

'Your bookkeeper?' says Squalida, astonished.

'He was Pepper's brother,' Luigi explains. 'I believe he stole the sphinx out of spite, but he paid a price for it. Not long ago, his body was found in the Bast.'

'So someone did him in, eh?' says Squalida. 'What's so special about this sphinx that people are willing to commit murder to get it?'

'Pepper told me that in the right hands, the sphinx is a source of immeasurable power,' Luigi says.

Squalida smiles like a greedy cat. 'Ooh, I like power!' she cries. 'Do go on, Luigi!'

CHAPTER TEN
A SHARING OF SECRETS

As Luigi Febbo embarks upon his frank discussion with Squalida MacHeath, back in 17, Scarlatti Mews, Crispin Rattle finds himself at a loose end. Returning from Malachi's upturned room, and still stumped, Callisto has gone out for a solitary stroll for the purposes of cogitation and Aril has slipped off somewhere. Consequently there is nothing for Crispin to do but mooch about. Ill-advisedly, he chooses the kitchen as the location for his mooching and Mrs Moncrief, who is floury and bustling, will brook no moochers in her domain. 'For goodness' sake get out from under my

feet before you cause a culinary mishap, Crispin Rattle!' she snaps. 'Go and do something.'

'Such as what, ma'am?' says Crispin.

'Read an improving book.'

Crispin's mouth turns down at the corners. 'I ain't much of a one for reading.'

'Write a letter then.'

'Ain't got no one to write to, have I?' says Crispin.

'Well how did you occupy your Sundays in London?' Mrs Moncrief demands.

'Me and some other lads would generally go for a lark about in the countryside, but there ain't no countryside round here for me to lark about in,' says Crispin. 'Can't I stay and help you?'

Mrs Moncrief snatches up a doughy wooden spoon and flourishes it like a royal sceptre. 'Completely and utterly not!' she says. 'Males and kitchens don't mix. Whenever the late Mr Moncrief tried to help me cook, my Yorkshires wouldn't rise and my dumplings boiled over. Why don't you join Miss Aril?'

'On account of how I don't know where she is, ma'am.'

With a sweeping gesture Mrs Moncrief points the spoon at the back door, and in the manner of a diva about to burst into an aria says, 'You will find her – in the garden!'

Back gardens tend to be small in Scarlatti Mews and Callisto's garden is no exception. Bounded on three sides by brick walls, it contains a lawn about the size of a tablecloth, and two narrow strips of soil which are presently putting on a display of snowdrops and crocuses.

Aril is seated cross-legged on the lawn. Her long hair has been tied back behind her head. She is dressed in a fisherman's sweater and baggy red trousers. Her palms are resting on her knees and her eyes are closed. There is a stillness about her that is like the silence inside a church, and Crispin almost tiptoes up to her. As quietly as he can, he sits facing her and whispers, 'What you doing?'

'Meditating,' says Aril.

'Oh!' Crispin says. 'Ain't that what doctors do?'

Aril opens her eyes; they are so deep that Crispin almost falls into them.

'Meditation is a way of soothing the spirit of life within you,' says Aril. 'When I meditate, I try to stop thinking so that my worries will go away.'

Crispin has trouble grasping this idea. 'Yeah, but your worries come back again as soon as you leave off, don't they?'

'Yes, but sometimes they don't seem so worrying,' says Aril.

She does not appear to mind Crispin's interruption, and he takes the opportunity to settle a few matters that he is curious about. 'How did you come to be Mr

Callisto's assistant?' he asks.

'We met in India five years ago,' says Aril. 'Callisto rescued me.'

'*Rescued* you?'

An unpleasant memory passes like a shadow across Aril's face. 'My parents died when I was little,' she says. 'I was driven out of the village where I lived and I went into the forest. I was happy there, until some hunters trapped me.'

Crispin frowns. 'How d'you mean, "trapped"?'

'They threw a net over me, pulled me to the ground and tied me up.'

Crispin makes his right hand into a fist and thumps the lawn with it. 'They wouldn't have done that to you if I'd been there!' he growls.

'After they captured me, they sold me to a man who owned a travelling circus,' continues Aril. 'He beat me cruelly and kept me in a cage. The circus toured the country, stopping in villages and towns.

103

The man charged people who wanted to look at me. Some laughed when they saw me, some called me names, but they all feared me.'

'You?' Crispin snorts in disbelief. 'Why would anyone be frightened of you?'

Aril smiles mysteriously. 'You wouldn't know because you've only seen me as I look now,' she says.

Crispin does not understand what Aril means, but he doesn't ask her about it because he is too eager to hear the rest of her story. 'Tell me about when you and Mr Callisto met,' he urges.

'I noticed him in the crowd one day,' says Aril. 'He stood out – and not just because of the colour of his skin. When he looked at me, there were tears in his eyes. He tried to buy my freedom, but the circus owner wouldn't sell me, so Callisto came back late at night, opened my cage and freed me. I ran away with him, and when we came back to Britain he made himself my guardian.'

'Is that like your father, type of thing?' Crispin says.

Aril nods. 'I owe him everything. I would lay down my life to protect him,' she says. Her voice is low and passionate; she means every word.

Now that Aril has trusted him with something of her secret self, Crispin feels honour-bound to return the compliment. 'I ain't been quite straight with you and Mr Callisto,' he reveals.

Though Aril suspected as much, she feigns a surprised expression. 'Really?'

'You know how I said my ma told me to come to Wolveston and find Mr Callisto?' Crispin says. 'Well that's true enough, but I left a part out.'

'What part?' says Aril.

'My ma told me after she was dead,' Crispin says.

'You see her in your dreams?'

'Yeah,' Crispin says, then adds in a

quieter voice, 'And sometimes when I'm awake and all. I never said nothing, 'cause I was scared that you and Mr Callisto might think I was a bit...you know.' Crispin taps the centre of his forehead with a finger.

'I don't think you're mad, and neither will Callisto,' says Aril. 'You must tell him what you've told me.'

'I will!' promises Crispin.

Aril stiffens. 'Callisto is on his way,' she says. 'He's just at the end of Pinchbeck Street.'

'Huh?' says Crispin. 'How d'you know that?'

'I can hear his footsteps,' Aril says.

Crispin thinks that Aril is having him on until, some five minutes or so later, Callisto arrives home.

CHAPTER ELEVEN
LOST PROPERTY

In the course of his long and thoughtful stroll, Callisto has made several deductions concerning the death of Malachi Pepper. Upon his return to Scarlatti Mews, the conjuror confers with Aril and Crispin around the dining table. Callisto listens carefully to what Crispin says about the manifestations of Rachel Rattle, and wonders if her appearances have any connection with the fate of her unfortunate brother.

'I said at breakfast that some aspects of the case of Malachi Pepper's murder intrigued me,' he tells Aril and Crispin, 'particularly the reward that Malachi's employer, Luigi Febbo, offered for information about his death.'

'That was generous of him!' Crispin remarks.

Callisto smiles grimly. 'I rather think not. Luigi Febbo's path and mine have crossed before. He's not a man much given to generosity, and seldom considers anyone but himself. He wants information, all right, but my intuition tells me he doesn't want information about Malachi's death.'

'What, then?' says Aril.

'It's my opinion that Malachi Pepper had something that Febbo desired, and that he hid it somewhere – that's what Febbo's after.'

'What's this bloke Febbo do, Mr Callisto?' Crispin enquires.

'He leads a double life,' replies Callisto. 'On the surface, he deals in antiquities – old jewels, parchments and the like. Below the surface, he's a handler of stolen goods. Envious collectors pay him to have things purloined from other collectors.'

The thought of such fraudulence excites Crispin's imagination. 'Maybe my uncle nicked something off of Febbo!' he speculates.

Callisto gives Crispin an admiring look. 'That's the very conclusion that I came to,' he says. 'I believe that Malachi Pepper concealed his theft and wrote a coded letter to Rachel Rattle that detailed its whereabouts.'

'Why would he do that?' Crispin says.

'For security,' says Callisto. 'I think that your uncle was afraid to return to the hiding place because he was being watched by someone who had an interest in the stolen object. Malachi needed someone on whom he could depend to collect the object and keep it safe. Who better than your mother, Crispin, and what place safer than London? But your mother was killed and your uncle was murdered before the plan could be executed.'

'Was Malachi Pepper murdered by Mr Febbo?' says Aril.

Callisto narrows his eyes. 'Hardly. Luigi Febbo is capable of many things, I don't doubt, but murder isn't one of them.'

'P'rhaps he hired someone to do the killing for him,' Crispin suggests.

'Why have him killed before he had revealed where the stolen object was?' says Callisto. 'No, Luigi Febbo is not the one. Another party is involved, someone capable of murder.'

'You could be right about Ma, you know,' Crispin says. 'Somebody was writing to her. She got letters regular for a few months before the accident.'

'Letters from whom?' asks Callisto.

'No idea,' Crispin says. 'She burned 'em in the grate as soon as she'd read 'em.' He laughs and runs his hand through his hair.

'Blimey, Mr Callisto!' he says. 'With a brain like yours, you ought to have been a detective.'

'I was, for a time,' Callisto admits, 'but I gave it up because of the long hours and low wages.'

There's a hint of pride in Aril's voice as she says, 'The police sometimes ask for Callisto's help.'

'Don't exaggerate!' Callisto scolds. 'The police have only asked for my assistance once or twice, in regard to cases where my areas of expertise seemed relevant.'

'And did you solve the cases, Mr Callisto?' says Crispin.

'I did,' Callisto admits reluctantly. 'But enough of the past – we have a puzzle of our own to solve.' He spreads out Crispin s letter on the dining table.

Crispin idly picks up the envelope and toys with it.

Callisto stares at the letters on the page.

K B Z L O K D K C F E H L
D P J V T L C Y P A D G N
I V A Z X K T E P G E C N

'Did your mother have a pet name that she liked to be called?' Callisto says.

'Not that I ever heard,' says Crispin.

'Was there a line of poetry, or a passage from the Bible that she was fond of quoting?'

Crispin laughs. 'What – Ma quote from the Bible? I should say not! She was dead set against churches and priests and that.'

'Ah yes!' Callisto agrees. 'Now that you mention it, I recall that she was.'

'She used to say that half the holy men in the world didn't know what they was on about, and the other half didn't know the half of what there was to be known,' declares Crispin.

Callisto and Aril trade fleeting glances when they hear this. Then Callisto says,

'Since we can't come upon the key phrase using logic, we must try a more round-about method of thinking. Let's suppose that the phrase forms part of the letter itself. If we all look at it and remark on any peculiarity we notice, we may stumble on something.'

After a couple of minutes, Aril says, 'The letter K is used more than any other, and M isn't used at all.'

'Nor is Q, R, S, U or W,' says Callisto, 'and there are no repeated sequences of letters.'

'What about replacing letters with numbers?' says Aril. 'One for A, two for B, and so on.'

'I have already tried and got nowhere,' Callisto says. 'Perhaps it's something more subtle – something in the ink or paper.' He holds the letter up to the light to see if there is a hallmark.

'Mr Callisto?' says Crispin.

'Hmm?'

'Have you noticed how part of the address on the envelope has been writ different than the rest?'

'In what way?' Callisto says.

Crispin turns the envelope around so that Callisto and Aril can inspect it. 'Look, Ma's name has been done in joined-up writing, but the rest is printed in capital letters.'

And Crispin is right. His mother's name has been inscribed in an elaborate copper-plate hand.

Callisto snaps his fingers. 'Of course! I was so busy poring over the letter that I didn't pay the envelope enough attention. Well done, Crispin Rattle!'

A tense half-hour follows. A grid is drawn up, twenty-six squares by twenty-six, and each square is filled with a letter of the alphabet. Once the grid is complete, Callisto writes *MRS RACHEL RATTLE* repeatedly above the coded message so that the first line reads:

M R S R A C H E L R A T T
K B Z L O K D K C F E H L

By carefully using the grid, Callisto reveals the following message.

WSR COMMONWEALTH BANK LEFT LUGGAGE LOCKER NINE

'What's WSR?' says Crispin.

'Wolveston Subterranean Railway,' Callisto informs him. 'Commonwealth Bank is one of its grandest stations. Your uncle concealed what he stole from Luigi Febbo there in a left luggage locker, where it still may be.'

'Unless the murderer forced Crispin's uncle to tell him before he killed him,' Aril says grimly.

'There's only one way to be sure,' says Callisto. He takes out a pocket watch and consults it. 'There's a limited service on Sunday, and I'll have to change onto the

Commonwealth Line at Fitzmoor Street, but even so I should be back within the hour.'

Aril makes to rise from her chair.

'No, Aril. I want you and Crispin to remain at home,' Callisto says. 'This might prove to be dangerous.'

'All the more reason for you to take me with you then,' says Aril. 'Don't you think an extra pair of *eyes* and *ears* and an extra *nose* might come in handy?'

'And if you're going, Aril, so am I!' says Crispin. 'I ain't stopping in on my own with Mrs Moncrief. She's liable to tidy me away and sling me out with the rubbish.'

Callisto raises the palms of both hands in a gesture of surrender. 'Very well!' he sighs. 'But if anything happens, I want no heroics. At the first sign of trouble, you're to run like rabbits – is that understood?'

'Yes!' Crispin and Aril say together.

* * *

Even though it is Sunday, there are a fair few people about, and there is standing-room only on the train between Bywater and Fitzmoor Street. From that station on, thankfully, the trains are less congested. The Commonwealth Line serves the banks and offices of Wolveston's commercial district, which is mostly shut at the week-end. Since there is nothing to see in the area but large, sombre buildings, and since there are no places of entertainment to be found within it, Wolvestonians tend to take their pleasures elsewhere.

Commonwealth Bank Station is soberly sumptuous. Its walls are decorated with portraits of past principals of the bank, made from glazed tiles, each portrait set in a golden-tiled frame. Fixtures and fittings have been tastefully painted banknote blue, and everything gleams and glints.

Crispin feels overawed, and if he were not with Callisto and Aril he would hurry out of the station, into the open air.

There are only two passengers waiting on the opposite, southbound platform: a young woman with a large hat and a small dog, and a portly gentleman who is engrossed in the current edition of the *Financial Reporter*.

'Aril?' Callisto murmurs.

Aril sniffs twice. 'They're no threat,' she says.

'How can you tell?' demands Crispin.

Here is Aril's mysterious smile again, a twin to the smile she gave Crispin in the garden earlier on. 'I have a sixth sense about these things,' she says.

Crispin's eyes widen. 'Here, you ain't a witch, are you?'

'No,' Callisto breaks in. 'Aril isn't a witch – she's far more interesting than that. Now follow me and stay close.'

Exit signs direct them into a long tunnel. At the far end of the tunnel they mount a steam staircase that takes them up to the station's main concourse, which is all wrought iron, mahogany and reddish-brown marble. The left luggage lockers are situated in a shadowy corner, partly screened from view by a row of pillars.

'Hang on, Mr Callisto, ain't them lockers locked?' says Crispin.

'Naturally.'

'So how you going to open Number Nine without a key?'

'Lack of a key will present us with no problem,' Callisto says confidently.

They come to the lockers. While Aril keeps watch, Callisto slips out a length of thin, springy wire that was concealed up his sleeve, pokes the wire into the lock of Number Nine and jiggles it about. There is a metallic snap and the door swings back to reveal a small leather grip, like a doctor's bag. The grip is secured with a brass padlock.

'We'll take this back to Scarlatti Mews at once,' says Callisto. He frowns. 'Aril? What is it?'

Aril is gazing at the grip, and her face twists in a spasm of fear and disgust.

'You feel something?' Callisto says.

'When you open that bag, wear gloves,' advises Aril. 'Don't touch what's inside with your bare skin.'

'Why not?'

'Because it's hungry,' Aril says.

From below their feet comes the rumble, hiss and shriek of an approaching train. It sounds like some gigantic metal beast mounting an attack.

CHAPTER TWELVE
ON THE WHEEL

Of all the famous landmarks in Wolveston, none is more famous than the Big Wheel. Standing on the north bank of the Bast, not far from the ruins of Wolveston Castle, the wheel has come to symbolize the city. Its image is to be found on the snowdomes, pencil sharpeners, tankards and plates that tourists buy as souvenirs. The wheel is recognized the world over as a modern wonder, and to visit Wolveston without riding on it is inconceivable.

This Sunday afternoon, the queue for the wheel stretches as far as Greenfield Butts, a distance of over half a mile.

In the queue's midst stands Jasper Pepper.

Jasper's face wears a preoccupied look, and his lips move as he mutters to himself. The demon's words echo through his brain. *It's not on the earth, or on the water, or under the water. It's hidden in plain view, in a place where many go but none stops.*

It has occurred to Jasper that the Big Wheel satisfies all these specifications, and he intends to take an investigatory ride. The fact that the size and structure of the wheel afford tens of thousands of potential hiding places does not daunt Jasper in the least. He places his trust in the special powers of sensitivity which he has developed, at no little cost to himself, to a remarkable degree. His patience, however, is not so developed. In the last half-hour the queue has progressed barely ten metres, and Jasper estimates that night will have fallen by the time his turn comes. This concerns him, since he has important ceremonies to perform and they must take place at sunset.

The Wolveston Big Wheel Company employs attendants to parade up and down the queues and keep order. Here comes one of them now, trudging like a clockwork soldier, wearing a black, brass-buttoned tunic, black trousers, a black stovepipe hat and a black truncheon in a holster on his belt. As he passes along, he utters a reassuring but inaccurate, 'Won't be long now.'

Jasper beckons to the attendant.

'Look here, my good fellow,' Jasper begins. 'I'm in rather a hurry, and I'd like you to escort me to the head of the queue, a service for which you will be handsomely recompensed.'

The attendant frowns. His dark eye-brows bristle and his bulbous nose twitches. 'Escort you to the front, sir? I don't know about that. My employers are pretty hot when it comes to that sort of thing, sir. They're sticklers for the rules.'

Jasper looks straight into the man's eyes and speaks in a deep, compelling voice. 'Listen closely to me. I am a Devon Court police officer. Here is proof of my identity.'

He opens his hand. Resting on his palm is a threepenny bit, but the attendant sees a brass badge bearing the arms of the Wolveston Civic Constabulary, a dragon rampant above the motto *Semper Vigilans*.

'I have reason to believe that a dangerous criminal will board the next ride on the wheel, and it is imperative that I follow him,' says Jasper. 'If he gives me the slip, months of painstaking investigation will have been in vain.'

The attendant straightens his shoulders. 'This way, sir!' he says briskly, and he leads Jasper forward.

Wolvestonians have a keen sense of justice – the last monarch of England had his head cut off on account of it – and

Jasper's progress does not go without comment. But when the attendant hears disparaging words, he points to his truncheon, raises a finger to his lips, and the matter is settled peacefully.

Jasper steps into a glass-fronted gondola and seats himself on a wooden bench. The gondola is intended to carry four, but when a woman and her two young sons attempt to enter, Jasper says, 'All the seats are taken.'

The woman blinks and says, 'So they are! I do beg your pardon.'

One of the boys says, 'But Mu-um—!' and the rest is lost as the door closes and the gondola rises so that the next comes up to the boarding platform.

The loading of the wheel seems an interminable process to most people, but Jasper does not mind it; he has not come here to enjoy himself. The gondola mounts higher and higher until

Wolverton is spread out like a counterpane. Jasper shuts his eyes, adjusts the rhythm of his breathing and allows his spirit to look at the city.

He sees a spangled web of coloured lights and each light is a pinprick point of belief. Cathedrals, churches, synagogues, mosques and Parsee towers are an insipid shade of puce. Law courts and the Parliament building are turquoise, and the Protector's Palace is cobalt blue. Scattered here and there are speckles of a rich ruby red, denoting gatherings of Jasper's fellow demonists.

He contracts his spiritual vision and projects it onto the wheel itself. There is nothing but cold iron and hot engines. Jasper can detect no trace of the power for which he is searching—

'You'll never find it with your spirit sight, Jasper!' says a voice at his side.

Jasper opens his eyes, turns his head and sees that the young woman he met in

Taffit Square has materialized next to him on the bench. 'What's this?' he snarls. 'I didn't send for you!'

'No, but I came anyway,' says the young woman. She taps Jasper's shoulder with a closed fan. 'Oh, Jasper! Let me indulge a little whim. You know how a lady likes to be unpredictable.'

'But you're no lady,' Jasper says scornfully.

The young woman laughs, allowing Jasper a glimpse of the inside of her mouth. Her tongue is as black as anthracite.

'What did you mean about my spirit sight?' Jasper says.

The young woman spreads her fan in front of her face and peers coquettishly over the top. 'The sphinx won't allow you to see it until it wants you to.'

'What nonsense is this?' Jasper barks. 'The sphinx cannot have wishes. It's an inanimate object, not a sentient being.'

'Is it now?' says the young woman, closing the fan again. 'If you know that, then you know more than I.'

Jasper becomes impatient. 'Why have you come to me?' he demands.

'To gloat,' says the young woman. 'Frustration and despair are meat and drink to me, and I mean to be slow over savouring yours. Say I used my demon arts to conjure the sphinx here, just this minute. What would you use it for, I wonder?'

Jasper waves his hand at the view from the gondola's window, and a vision comes to him. 'I would open all the portals of Inferno and infest this world with demons,' he says. 'Diabolic hordes would stalk the streets of Wolveston, slaughtering and feeding. The gutters would run red with gore. I would raise the dead to persecute the living. Innocence and love would have no meaning, only corruption and terror would prevail. The rich and mighty would bow down before me and beg for mercy that I would not allow them.'

The vision fades to silence.

'Poor, poor Jasper!' says the young woman. 'You lost your new toy before you even had a chance to play with it, didn't you?'

'That was my brother's doing – perdition take him!' Jasper curses.

The young woman wriggles her shoulders. 'Ah, anger!' she purrs. 'How invigorating! But you'll be gratified to learn that your lost toy remains in the family. Your nephew has found it.'

Jasper's face is a mask of incomprehension. 'What the deuce does my nephew have to do with it?' he splutters.

'Your nephew has a great deal to do with it,' says the young woman. 'He's a pleasant enough lad, but I don't approve of the company he keeps.'

Jasper recognizes that the demon is

deliberately provoking him. With difficulty he quells the tide of fury that is
rising inside him, and he keeps his voice
calm as he says, 'Really? What company
would that be?'

'A man, a young girl and a housekeeper,'
the young woman says airily. 'You can
see the neighbourhood as plain as plain
from here.'

'You mean that the boy is in Wolveston?'
says Jasper.

'You must never ask a lady what she
means, Jasper,' the young woman advises.
'Her reply is bound to be deceiving. It's
such a shame that I won't tell you
Crispin's address, and even more of a
shame that it's impossible for you to
compel me to tell you. A man could
spend his whole life searching for someone in Wolveston. But suppose I relented
and revealed to you where your nephew is
living, what would you think?'

'I would naturally assume that you were

lying in order to torment me with false hopes,' says Jasper. 'But knowing that I would make such an assumption, you might well tell me the truth in a way that would lead me to discount it. However, were I to believe that you had told me the truth in the form of a lie and I acted on that lying truth, I would discover it to be a true lie.'

'Oh, Jasper!' sighs the young woman. 'I have you in the most exquisite tangle.' The twinkle leaves her eyes. 'You'll have to account to me in the end, Jasper,' she says. 'Words can't express how keenly I'm look-ing forward to it. I'll show you chasms whose inhabitants would welcome pain as a relief from their suffering. Shall I tell you a secret, Jasper?'

'If I said no, would it stop you?' Jasper enquires dryly.

'All human endeavour is pointless,' says the young woman. 'All life is futile. The Universe has no meaning. At the end of hope, fear, love and hatred is an endless black nothing that engulfs everything and endures beyond for ever.'

The young woman's words paint a picture in Jasper's mind. He sees the vast darkness and feels his identity beginning to leak away. 'I am real!' he says. 'This seat is real! The city, the sky and the air I breathe are real. You are not real.'

The young woman raises her eyebrows. 'This world is real and I am not – or is it the other way round?' she says, and vanishes.

Chapter Thirteen
Communing with the Dead

All the way back to Scarlatti Mews, Callisto has the disagreeable sensation of being accompanied, as though someone were walking invisibly at his side. He is sure that the sensation emanates from the grip that he carries, though outwardly there is nothing remarkable about it. Its leather is scuffed in some places and dotted with spots of grease in others. The brass padlock that fastens it is familiar, for Callisto has modified several padlocks of the same design to use in the performance of tricks on stage. The grip is neither heavy nor light, but what it lacks in

weight it more than makes up for in presence.

Aril is as uneasy as Callisto, and she is careful to position herself so that there is no possibility of her accidentally bumping into the grip or brushing against it. She sensed something ancient and malign inside it, something she called 'hungry', but hunger comes nowhere near the longing and loneliness that she felt. Aril's instincts warn her of danger, and she has to make a conscious effort not to react violently to the warning.

Crispin is unhappily aware of his companions' discomfort and fears that he is to blame for it. He almost wishes that he had torn up the blessed letter and stayed in London, but if he had, he would not have met Aril. The London girls of his acquaintance have tended to be giggly. They go about in twos and threes, making up games with elaborate rules and showing no interest whatsoever in worthwhile pursuits, such as shouting, climbing trees, tussling and collecting frogspawn. Aril is entirely unlike any girl that Crispin has encountered. There is something different about her that sets her apart. Crispin cannot yet define what that difference is, but he wishes to. Indeed, he yearns to know everything that there is to know about Aril, and he dares to hope that they might become friends. He is, naturally, curious about the contents of the grip, but the satisfaction of his curiosity must be postponed, for when he, Callisto and Aril arrive home, they find that tea is waiting for them, and Mrs Moncrief insists that they seat themselves around the table at once.

'The taking of meals at regular intervals is the key to good health and a sound mind,' she informs them.

No one has the courage to disagree with her.

* * *

At last tea is over. The plates of sandwiches and scones have been emptied, the yellow moon of sponge cake has been sliced half-full. As Mrs Moncrief clears the table, Callisto compliments her. 'Another delicious meal, Mrs M. I don't know how you do it.'

'By means of hard work and diligence, Mr Callisto,' Mrs Moncrief replies. 'The kitchen is, in a manner of speaking, a small theatre in which I am called upon to act out everything from the light comedy of an iced dainty to the heartbreaking tragedy of ... of ...' The metaphor fails her.

'Where your cooking is concerned, there are no tragedies, Mrs M,' Callisto says gallantly. 'All your performances have happy endings.'

Mrs Moncrief exits with a blush the colour of cream of tomato soup.

The moment has come. Callisto retrieves the grip from beneath the table and rests it on his lap. From his sleeve he extracts the wire that he used at Commonwealth Bank Station and in the space of a minute both the padlock and the grip are open. Callisto dons a pair of gloves, reaches into the grip and removes an object that he places on the table.

It is a figurine, some twenty centimetres long by twelve centimetres high. The figurine has the body of a lion, the wings of an eagle and the face of a man wearing a head-dress with a cobra crest. The lion is in repose, its tail curled lazily round its right haunch. The wings are slightly raised. The man's eyes stare straight ahead. The figurine has been carved from a black stone speckled with silvery flecks that reflect the light and give a shimmering effect.

'A sphinx!' Callisto mutters. 'A black sphinx.'

'My uncle got himself murdered over a piece of junk like that?' Crispin says incredulously. 'He must have got the crackers something chronic!'

'Or perhaps not,' says Callisto. 'This sphinx may be—'

And all at once the sphinx shows what it may be. The colours of the room drain into the stone figure and its blackness gleams, radiating shadows. Each one of the three seated around the dining table sees something different, is taken to a different place.

Crispin is beside the River Thames. To his right lies a broad meadow. A breeze blows, silvering the rippling grass with the light of the sun. Dandelions bob and twitch. To Crispin's left, mallard ducks swim against the current, paddling furiously to stay fixed in the same spot.

Rachel Rattle rises up out of the water and clambers onto the bank. Her clothes are wet, muddy, ruined. Green weed is tangled in her hair. Her eyes are misty, like the eyes of a fish that has lain too long on a fishmonger's slab. 'I was wrong, Crispin,' she says.

'Wrong about what, Ma?'

'Life,' Rachel says. 'I wasted mine. The only good I ever did was on the day that you were born. Now look at me! It goes on for ever, you know, being dead. There's no letup. You live your life to the full, Crispin – no second-bests. Follow what makes you happy and don't lose track of it.'

'I won't, Ma,' says Crispin. 'But this ain't right, is it? We shouldn't be talking this way. I ought to be with Mr Callisto and Aril, and you ought to be lying peaceful in your grave.'

'The Black Sphinx brought me back, and took you to Wolveston,' Rachel says. 'The Black Sphinx has a mind and plans of its own. I should never have listened to Malachi! He promised me money. He wrote that if I took the sphinx and hid it in London, it would be a prank, like the ones we used to play when we were children. You don't get many chances to play games when you're a grown-up, Crispin. I seized the chance and believed Malachi, but he lied to me. It wasn't a game. He stole the sphinx out of spite, and then he wanted to get rid of it because he was afraid of what it showed him. He wanted to pass its curse on to me!'

The anguish in his mother's voice goes right through Crispin.

'How can I help, Ma?' he says. 'What can I do?'

Rachel's eyes take on a distant expression.

'You might be the only one who can help, Crispin,' she says. 'The sphinx wants to be free, but it can only be set free by someone who can see it for what it is.'

Crispin frowns. Rachel's voice seems to have changed, and now her figure starts to flicker like a candle-flame in a draught. Between the flickers, Crispin almost makes out someone shorter and slighter standing before him.

'You ain't her, are you?' he whispers. 'You ain't my ma!'

He is returned to the dining room without a reply.

The moment that Aril set eyes on the sphinx, she felt it call to her blood and her blood responded. She has been plunged into a tropical forest. All around her is greenery and gloom. The hot and heavy air is filled with the whirring, whining and chittering of insects. She would appear to be in India, or in her memories of it.

Aril remains still, listens and watches. She does not know how she comes to be in this place, or whether it is real or not, but she knows that speculation would be fruitless. If she fails to adapt to her surroundings, she may not survive.

Details emerge. On the ground, ten metres in front of her, a brown snake basks in a patch of sunlight. Each of the snake's coils is as thick as Aril's forearm. The serpent flicks out its forked tongue to taste her scent. A slender brook of ants teems up and down the trunk of a near-by tree. A bird cackles overhead. From behind her comes the rustle of leaves in a non-existent breeze, the noise of moss springing back into place after being stepped on, air passing in and out of lungs.

Aril breathes in through her nose and catches a distinctive smell, a combination of vinegar, burnt-out fireworks and sweet spices. A predator is stalking her, creeping closer and closer, betraying itself with a drawn-out growl that rattles in its throat.

Without turning, Aril says, 'Hello, Father,' and she is in the dining room again.

Callisto finds himself within stone walls that enclose a darkness so cavernous, the torches blazing in their brackets cannot illuminate it all. Light wavers over carved hieroglyphs. The air smells of incense. One of the torches sputters, its flame twitches, and a shadow falls across the floor at Callisto's feet, the shadow of a man with a jackal's head.

A voice speaks wordlessly in the language of the mind. 'Who approaches the gates?'

Callisto is uncertain of what to say, but estimates that humility will not come amiss. 'One of the unworthy,' he says.

'What is it that you seek?'

'Questions,' Callisto says. 'All wisdom proceeds from the asking of questions. To grow wise I must first learn what questions to ask.'

The dark resounds with the hint of a laugh that would grind mountains into dust. 'You have a honeyed tongue, unworthy one. Why should I open my gate for the likes of you?'

'Because it might please you to do so,' Callisto says.

The laugh comes again. The torch-flames flinch away from it like whipped dogs. 'Do not trouble me with your insolence in future, unworthy one.'

The shadow on the floor merges with the dark.

Callisto hears footsteps, the slapping of bare feet on stone. A wild-haired woman dressed in a shroud stumbles into the light. She is dead. Her eyes are black; her mouth is filled with shadow; her voice is as dry as sand. 'Why did you bring me here?'

Callisto's face is wet with tears. 'I'm sorry!' he says. 'I didn't know that it would be you.'

'Who else?' says the woman. 'I heard the half of you that is me. How could I not answer?'

Callisto holds out both his hands. 'I tried,' he says. 'Before you died, I did my best to—'

'No time for that,' the woman interrupts. 'Go to the living for praise or blame. You told me that I was a fool and you were right, but I wouldn't listen. I thought I could contain the demon and manage it. Instead it managed me and destroyed me utterly. It has a thousand faces, a thousand cunnings.'

'I will avenge you!' Callisto vows.

'No!' cries the woman. 'Bazimaal is too strong a demon for you.'

'I want you to find peace,' Callisto says.

'More like you'll bring down torment on us both,' says the woman. 'Leave me. You remind me of the world, and that's the worst torment of all. Abandon magic. Marry, have children, lead an ordinary life.'

'No,' says Callisto.

The woman, the walls and the torches are no longer there. Callisto sees the dining room, the black sphinx, Aril and Crispin. He breathes deeply to keep himself from sobbing.

* * *

Callisto, Aril and Crispin have joined hands, for they all feel in need of a little warm human contact.

'It was real as anything!' says Crispin. 'I was by the river, just outside London, and Ma was there. I asked if I could help her, and she told me the sphinx wanted to be free, and then it was like she wasn't herself any more.'

'Who was she?' says Callisto.

Crispin cannot put the strangeness of what he witnessed into words, and shakes his head.

'I don't know,' he confesses. 'Who did you see, Mr Callisto?'

Callisto stiffens slightly.

'My mother, walking in the Halls of the Dead,' he says.

There is a prickliness about him that suggests it would not be wise to question him further.

'And I was in India with my father, but

I didn't see him,' Aril says. 'He was hunting me.'

'You're sure it was your father?' says Callisto.

'I recognized his scent,' says Aril.

Crispin is tempted to comment on the notion of Aril's father wearing scent, but he restrains himself.

'And he was in his, er, alternative form?' Callisto enquires delicately.

'He was as I remember him best,' says Aril. She wrinkles up her nose. 'The sphinx took control of us. We must destroy the thing – it's evil!'

'It has a power that may possibly be put to evil use, but equally may be used to do good,' Callisto says. 'We should learn more about it before we decide what's to be done with it.'

A heated discussion follows, in which Callisto is reasonable, Aril is unreasonable and Crispin is out of his depth. The discussion terminates when Aril flies from the room, slamming the door behind her.

'Got a temper on her, ain't she?' remarks Crispin.

'She is concerned and, I think, a little afraid,' says Callisto. 'But come, Crispin, let's distract ourselves from all this sombreness. Do you play draughts?'

'A bit,' says Crispin.

And so the afternoon passes into evening. Her fit of pique over, Aril reappears, declares that draughts is a game fit only for babies and announces her intention to teach Crispin the basics of chess.

Callisto avails himself of the opportunity to go up to his room and consult his books, for he has many questions that he would like answered. He takes the sphinx with him, locked in the grip, and places it at the back of his wardrobe. As he does, possibilities occur to him. They coil like smoke, elusive and fascinating. Since chance has brought the sphinx to him, why not learn how to tame its power and use it to be revenged on the demon who took his mother's life? He imagines the hot satisfaction this would give him, and then—

Callisto chuckles dryly.

'Oh, you *are* dangerous, aren't you?' he says to the sphinx. 'I'll have to watch my step *and* my thoughts when I'm around you.'

CHAPTER FOURTEEN
IN THE MUSEUM

On Monday morning, bright and early, Mrs Moncrief and Aril take Crispin shopping. Before she leaves Scarlatti Mews, Mrs Moncrief retrieves a formidably large umbrella from the hall stand. The umbrella is black, with a white bone handle that has been shaped into the likeness of a goose's head and neck.

'You won't be needing no umbrella, ma'am,' says Crispin. 'Sun's shining fit to bust outside.'

Mrs Moncrief blinks slowly and says, with great dignity, 'The sunshine does not signify, Crispin Rattle. A lady's umbrella is more than just protection from the elements, it is an expression of her character. Were I to leave this house without mine, I should feel improperly dressed.'

Aril shoots Crispin a knowing look; he manages to turn his snigger into a cough.

The morning's shopping begins, naturally enough, in Everett Row, whose tailors are renowned for the quality of their work. Mrs Moncrief conducts Aril and Crispin to the premises of Broadstone and Meeker, among whose customers are, as the dragon crest on their sign proudly attests, Lord Protector Groves and his family.

Before the bell above the door of the shop has ceased its jingling, an assistant appears. He is a thin, dark young man who looks unscrupulously clean. His primped oily hair is matched by his primped oily smile – but when the assistant catches sight of Crispin's clothes, his face pales and his smile turns to a horrified grimace. 'Has the young man been involved in an accident?' he enquires.

'No, he is a Londoner,' Mrs Moncrief informs him. 'I wish him to be transformed, to be brought to the very acme of fashion.'

'I'll try my best, madam,' says the assistant, in the tone of one who has been given a sow's ear and ordered to make a silk purse of it.

There follows a lengthy spell during which Crispin is prodded, poked, measured and tutted over until he is quite dazed. He thanks goodness for Aril, who gives her honest opinion of the clothes he tries on. At last they decide on a brown corduroy Norfolk jacket, striped woollen trousers, black boots and a tweed overcoat with a matching flat cap. When Crispin studies his reflection in a full-length looking-glass, he declares, 'Swipe me! Don't I look a toff?'

The assistant leans deferentially closer to

Mrs Moncrief and murmurs, 'How would madam like to pay?'

Mrs Moncrief holds her umbrella aloft as if it were the Sword of Truth. 'Charge the items to the account of Mr Callisto!' she declares grandly.

The assistant, overcome with awe, can do no more than nod.

While his account at Broadstone and Meeker is being charged, back in Scarlatti Mews, Callisto is passing a trying morning after passing a trying night before. He has pored over his entire collection of books in an attempt to find the origins of the Black Sphinx, but has not come across a single reference to it, not even in Dr John Dee's *Sundries of Magic*. Though he is anxious to keep the existence of the sphinx as secret as possible, Callisto recognizes that he needs the advice of an expert on ancient Egyptian artefacts; happily he knows just the person. He takes a sheet of paper and a pencil and, from memory, makes a sketch of the sphinx. He intends to use the sketch for reference purposes, judging that the sphinx is too risky an object to be carried across Wolveston. In fact Callisto now considers the sphinx to be so risky that he would rather not handle it at all. Such sleep as he managed during the night was disturbed by dreams in which the sphinx tested and tempted him.

Shortly after the sketch is finished, the shopping expedition party returns, and Crispin parades so that Callisto can admire him. 'I congratulate you on your refined taste,' says Callisto.

'It weren't my taste, Mr Callisto,' Crispin confesses. 'It was mostly Aril what did the choosing. I've been wondering how I'm going to pay you for this lot. These togs didn't come cheap.'

'Oh, we'll think of something!' Callisto says dismissively. 'In the meantime, would you care to come with me after lunch?'

'Where to?'

'First to the Egyptian Hall,' says Callisto, 'and then to see a man about a sphinx.'

At the Egyptian Hall, Crispin makes himself as useful as he can while Callisto carries out an inspection of the apparatus that will be used during this evening's performance. Crispin was previously unaware that the making of magic involved so many ropes and wires, straps and springs, bolts and hinges, all of which Callisto carefully checks.

'Don't you ever get fed up of this lark, Mr Callisto?' says Crispin.

'It's a tedious but vital chore,' Callisto explains. 'If I am negligent of any detail, it could put Aril or myself in danger.' He examines a clip on a flying-harness. 'That should see us right for tonight,' he says. 'Let's be off to Totteridge Square.'

Totteridge Square, which is a ten-minute

walk from the Egyptian Hall, is the location of the National Museum. The 'Nash', as it is affectionately known, is built of limestone blocks and rises in a series of terraces, after the manner of the Ziggurat of Ur. On the topmost terrace stands a silvered disc, positioned so as to catch the first rays of the dawning sun at the summer and winter solstices.

The museum houses archaeological and artistic treasures from around the globe, all legally obtained at a fair price. The barbaric practice of invading other nations and plundering their cultural heritage was stopped at about the same time that the monarchy was abandoned.

In the foyer of the museum, Callisto hands his visiting card to an attendant and asks for Professor Lyons.

Crispin glances around, sees bits of broken statues and brownish paintings in gilt frames, and is not quite sure what to make of them.

'I'm sure Professor Lyons will see us, for he and I are old acquaintances,' says Callisto. 'I think it would be better if you left the talking to me, Crispin.'

'Right you are!' Crispin chirrups. 'How come you know a professor in a museum, Mr Callisto?'

Callisto smiles. 'Professor Lyons is a keen amateur conjuror. He asked me for lessons, and under my guidance has progressed to the point where he is much in demand at children's parties. He goes by the name of the Astounding Supremo.'

Crispin scratches his head in bafflement – conjurors who are detectives, antique dealers who traffic in stolen goods, professors who are conjurors – is no one in Wolveston what they seem?

The attendant returns with the message that the professor will be pleased to receive Callisto straight away.

Balthasar Lyons, curator of the Ancient

Egyptian Department of the National Museum, is of medium height, stocky build and is aged sixty or thereabouts. His eyes, magnified by the lenses of his spectacles until they are almost saucer-sized, are blue, his beard is white, his hair is entirely absent and his bald head is as glossy as a hawthorn berry. His office is cramped, cluttered and fusty.

Callisto and the professor greet each other cordially. The professor asks after Aril and, as he puts it, 'the inestimable Mrs Moncrief'. Then he turns a quizzical eye on Crispin.

'This is Crispin Rattle,' Callisto says. 'He's the son of an old friend.'

Crispin gives the old gentleman a wink.

'Do be seated, both of you,' Professor Lyons says. 'How may I be of assistance?'

Callisto produces the pencil sketch of the sphinx, shows it to the professor and says, 'Have you ever come across the like of that, Professor?'

Professor Lyons starts in his chair. 'By Jove, what a singular coincidence!' he cries. 'Two months ago a colleague in Russia sent me a query regarding an object almost identical to this, and I have been researching it ever since.' He indicates a tumble of books and papers on his desk. The untidy heap resembles the aftermath of a library avalanche.

'You know all about it, then,' says Callisto.

The professor smiles. 'I know of it, my dear chap, but I'd hesitate to assert that I know *all* about it. Some of what I have turned up can be considered hard fact, the rest is superstition and confabulation.'

'Would it be presumptuous of me to ask if you would be willing to share a little of the harvest of your knowledge?' says Callisto.

Though Professor Lyons is embarrassed by direct flattery, he can stand no end of implied flattery and he positively preens as he declaims, 'The Black Sphinx, as it has come to be known over the ages, originated in the distant past, approximately four and a half thousand years ago. It was made in Egypt during the reign of the pharaoh Djoser by Imhotep, the pharaoh's vizier, architect and Chief of the Royal Magic Secrets. The sphinx was said to have been buried with Imhotep, but five centuries after his death his grave was looted by tomb robbers. I can find no further reference to the sphinx until the twelfth century, when it is listed in the inventory of a Knights Templar castle in Malta. From there, it seems—'

Callisto notices that Crispin's eyes have turned glassy. 'Forgive me, Professor,' he says gently, 'but I don't want to take up too much of your afternoon. Do you know anything of the more recent history of the sphinx?'

'I do,' says Professor Lyons. 'In November of last year an object purported to be the Black Sphinx was stolen from a cabinet in the Winter Palace Museum at St Petersburg. Of course, it is most unlikely that it was the *actual* sphinx, since such artefacts rarely survive, unfortunately.'

'But suppose it were the true Black Sphinx,' says Callisto. 'What significance would it have?'

'As an example of Third Dynasty craftsmanship, enormous significance!' the professor says.

'You misunderstand me,' says Callisto. 'Perhaps I should have asked you for what purpose the sphinx was first made.'

Professor Lyons snorts derisively. 'To do that, I'm afraid I should have to enter into the realms of the supernatural and fantastical. All that mumbo-jumbo is so much rot to a scientist like myself.'

'Indulge me!' insists Callisto.

The professor is suddenly wary. He raises his left eyebrow. 'Why are you suddenly so interested in the Black Sphinx, Callisto?'

'It was mentioned in the course of a conversation with a friend,' says Callisto. 'I want to know the sphinx's story because I fancy I might work it up for a stage act – *The Mysteries of the Pharaoh* – quite fitting for the Egyptian Hall, I'm sure you'll agree.'

This oblique reference to conjuring puts a shine in the professor's eyes. 'Anything for a fellow prestidigitator, eh?' He leans back in his chair. 'The story goes that Imhotep invested the sphinx with a considerable proportion of his magic powers, and sacrificed his own son in order to bind those powers and confine them. He held that the sphinx made it possible to link the world of the living with the demon world of Inferno.'

'*What?*' rasps Callisto.

'Legend has it that Imhotep used the sphinx to talk to dead people, and demons.' The professor laughs. 'Did you ever hear such nonsense?'

Callisto's face turns pale. 'No,' he mumbles, 'no indeed. Thank you for your assistance. Is there something I might do for you in return?'

The professor laughs in a somewhat embarrassed way. 'In my extracurricular studies, I happened upon something called "the cat and mango trick". Do you know anything about it?'

Now it is Callisto's turn to give a lecture; Crispin's eyes grow as glazed as a ship's porthole.

Chapter Fifteen
On Constitution Row

Jasper Pepper does not look his usual dapper self. His hair is lank, his cheeks are stubbled, his eyes are fever-bright and his clothes are creased. It is over twenty-four hours since he last slept and longer since he ate. He spent Sunday night in contemplation, observing rituals and burning Tibetan herbs and mosses on a small brazier in order to inhale their fumes. At sunrise he performed a geomantic divination which has brought him here to Constitution Row, a part of Parliament Park. The results of the divination urged Jasper to consider a change of scenery and a change of demon, and he expects a diabolical encounter.

Constitution Row is a broad avenue lined with lime trees and is popular among the leisured classes, who use it to exercise their dogs and horses or to meet their lovers in secret – especially at dusk. But there will be no trysting today. For all the blue sky and bright sunshine, the wind has an icy edge.

Jasper is unaware of the cold and scarcely knows where he is. To him, Wolveston is a ghostly city, sculpted in mist, woven in gossamer by tiny spiders. Only his desire for the sphinx seems solid, as hot and solid as newly cast iron. He can no longer remember a time when he was not seeking it, and has lost count of the number of occasions it has led him astray. This latest setback, which began when the sphinx was whisked away almost as his fingers were closing round it, has been singularly hard for Jasper to bear since it was his own brother who thwarted him.

Malachi, he thinks. Malachi and Rachel. Rachel and Malachi.

Memories flash before him: Malachi and Rachel giggling together in a corner; Malachi and Rachel passing each other coded messages; Malachi and Rachel laughing at a private joke made at Jasper's expense.

'Always together!' Jasper murmurs. 'Always close! Always sharing!'

Another memory occurs to him, an accidental meeting with Malachi, face to face in Trickler Street with no chance for either of them to ignore the other. Malachi automatically offers Jasper his right hand. Jasper regards the hand as though it were holding a wet fish.

'You're looking well and prosperous, Jasper,' Malachi says.

'And you look ill and down at heel,' Jasper replies coldly.

'There's no need to take that attitude with me,' says Malachi.

Jasper laughs. 'With you, Malachi, it is the *only* attitude to take. Still grubbing away at that seedy accountant's?'

'I may have a new employer soon,' Malachi confides. 'I've heard of an opening for a clerk in an import-export business.'

'I suppose that I could be less interested if I tried, but you're not worth the effort, Malachi,' Jasper says. 'Should you happen to notice me in the street again, be good enough to cross over to the other side.' He tries to step round Malachi, but Malachi shifts to block his way.

'Hold on a moment, Jasper. I think you should know that I have been in touch with Rachel recently. We write to each other regularly. She lives in London. I could let you have her address, if you like.'

'No, I do not like!' Jasper says scornfully. 'Rachel was a brat when she was a child, grew into a hussy and now, no doubt, is a fishwife. The only favour she ever granted me was leaving my life and I would be gratified if you were to render me the same kindness, Malachi . . .'

The memory fades into the blueness of the sky, and Jasper speculates. Rachel and Malachi, Malachi and Rachel. What was the nature of their correspondence? Did they re-establish the intimacy that they shared in childhood? Perhaps Malachi wrote about his new employer, Luigi Febbo, and Jasper's visits to Febbo's shop. Perhaps Malachi told Rachel about the sphinx.

It is not the first, nor even the hundredth time that Jasper has thought along these mental railway lines that arrive at no terminus. He knows that his nephew has the sphinx and he knows that his nephew is in Wolveston, but as far as finding the boy is concerned, he might as well be in Outer Mongolia. Jasper has considered hiring a private detective, but they are too like policemen for his liking.

Despite all his experiences to the contrary, Jasper believes that he can outwit a demon into doing his work for him.

'Course, you know what the trouble is, don't you, guv?' says a gravelly voice, which brings Jasper back to Constitution Row and the present. 'You been mixing with the wrong sort.'

A tramp is strolling alongside Jasper, bizarrely dressed in tattered evening clothes. His opera hat has a broken brim and the top of its crown is missing. There are no toe caps on his boots. His face is almost entirely obscured by a grizzled beard and a pair of spectacles with dark-blue lenses. He smells of dirt, drains and damnation. His skin still shimmers with the heat of the regions from which he has lately sprung.

Jasper intuits that this must be the demonic encounter predicted in his divination.

'Have I?' he says.

'Ho yes!' says the tramp. 'You been mixing with Bazimaal, and Bazimaal's a sly and slippery customer.'

'So I have observed,' says Jasper.

'Lead you in a merry dance, will Bazimaal. Crooked as a country lane.'

'Unfortunately, having fallen into company with Bazimaal, I'm finding it difficult to fall out,' admits Jasper. 'What would you advise?'

The tramp scratches the back of his neck and sucks his teeth. 'Bazimaal's scared of the sphinx, you might make something of that.'

'Scared?' says Jasper, surprised.

'It's scared that once you've got the sphinx, you'll be able to use its power to master any demon. Bazimaal was a slave once, and it didn't like it. With the sphinx, you'd have the whip hand,' the tramp says.

'But I'm without the sphinx,' says Jasper.

'And that's the thing, ain't it, guv? How

to come by what destiny means you to
have – how to find the boy?'

Jasper's gaze sweeps across the misty
city. 'How shall I find the boy? Can you
tell me where he is?'

'I can, but I won't,' the tramp says. 'You
can't change demon nature, guv, no more
than you can milk a shark. We can't tell
the truth out straight to save our lives, if
we had lives that could be saved. Shadows
and lies, that's us. The best I can offer you
is a step along the road.'

'The right road?' Jasper says hopefully.

'You won't know that until you reach
the end of it,' says the tramp. 'Now I know
it's not my place to give you orders, but
think a minute, guv. The boy's in
Wolveston, right?'

Jasper nods.

'So he must have come for a reason,' says
the tramp.

'To visit someone he knows?' Jasper
ventures.

The tramp begins a throaty chuckle that ends as a racking cough. 'Wrong turning, guv!' he wheezes. 'London born and bred, that boy is. How could a yokel lad from London get to know anyone in Wolveston?'

'Someone his parents knew?' Jasper says.

'More particular than that, guv.'

'Someone his *mother* knew!' Jasper declares triumphantly.

'You might be right, guv, but there again you might not,' says the tramp. 'That's all the helping hand you'll get from me. I'm off.'

'Wait!' Jasper pleads. 'I don't know your name, or how to summon you.'

'Get the sphinx and you can have your pick of any one of us, guv,' says the tramp. 'Get the sphinx and Inferno's your oyster.' He turns and walks away.

Jasper continues thoughtfully in the opposite direction.

The tramp shuffles along Constitution

Row for a minute or so, then steps aside into a copse of linden trees. Here he meets the stylish young woman who has recently been keeping company with Jasper Pepper. The tramp and the young woman chirrup together in a demon dialect that contains neither vowels nor consonants.

'How was that, Bazimaal?' the tramp demands.

'Superb!' enthuses the young woman. 'Though this is almost too easy to be fun. Jasper is so full of self-deceit that one hardly has to try to mislead him. One merely winds him up and lets him go, like a clockwork toy.'

The tramp digs something out of his beard, cracks it between the nails of his index finger and thumb and flicks it away.

'Is it me, or is crossing the threshold into this world easier than it used to be?' he says.

'That is the sphinx's doing,' says the young woman. 'It's flexing its muscles.'

The tramp's frown is deep enough to be a grimace.

'What's the sphinx after, anyroad?' he says.

'Precisely the right sort of people,' says the young woman. 'They're like the numbers of a combination lock – they mean nothing on their own, but put them together in the right order, and Fanny's your aunt!'

The tramp smiles nostalgically.

'I knew a woman named Fanny once,' he says. 'She made me a lovely pie. I chopped her up and put her into it myself.'

A cab waits outside the gates of Parliament Park. The cabby has left his seat and is slouching with his back against the side of the cab. The man looks like a shaved ape: shallow-chinned, thick-browed, flat-nosed. His shoulders are broad and the muscles of his arms bulge in the sleeves of his coat. He spies Jasper approaching and straightens up. As Jasper passes him, the cabby says, 'Name of Pepper?'

Jasper stops, looks the man up and down. 'What of it?'

'Jasper Pepper?'

'*Mr* Pepper to you, my man!' Jasper says indignantly.

'Ain't your man though, am I?' says the cabby. 'Wants to see you, doesn't she?'

'Who?'

'My boss.'

'And who is your boss?' Jasper demands.

'Squalida MacHeath.' says the cabby. '*Miss* MacHeath to you. Hop in, I'm driving you.'

Jasper, like most of the other inhabitants of Wolveston, knows Squalida MacHeath by reputation, and takes a step back. 'Please convey my sincerest regrets to Miss MacHeath and assure her that I look forward to meeting her at a future date, but just now is not convenient.'

'Broken arm ain't convenient either, but that's what you'll get if you don't come with me,' says the cabby. 'It's taken me all night and most of the morning to find you and I ain't happy. Squalida's not fussed what condition you're in, so long as you're breathing and you can talk.'

Jasper bows to the inevitable. Just before he opens the door of the cab, he says, 'Have you any idea why Miss MacHeath wishes to see me?'

'She don't discuss her business with me, does she?' says the cabby. 'But I guess that if you've got money, you'll have less of it by the end of the day. If you ain't got money, you're bound for a trip to hospital or a funeral parlour.'

Jasper curls his top lip in a sneer. 'If you're attempting to intimidate me, you're not succeeding.'

'Takes all kinds,' says the cabby.

Chapter Sixteen
St Augustine's

The cab carrying Jasper Pepper has entered the Scarp, and is proceeding along Gospelmaker Road, Broadway's shoddy twin. It was once a wealthy commercial area, but its fine buildings are now in an advanced stage of decay and have a pouched, baggy look. The cracked, uneven pavements are packed with costermongers, cardsharps and grimy children whose faces are old beyond their years. Barrel-organs jangle. Brawls burst the confines of taverns and spill out onto the road. Life here is soiled and shabby, lived at a full shout or a fervent whisper. Among these narrow streets and twining alleyways money can buy anything, for everything is for sale – on special offer at bargain rates. Wolveston is the greatest city on earth, but the Scarp is its deepest shame.

Jasper looks out of the cab's window and is transfixed. He has been to the Scarp on many occasions, but never by day. The seediness of the surroundings and the despondency he sees in face after face excite him. It occurs to him that once the sphinx is his and he has learned how to control its power, the Scarp will be a hunting-ground for demons, who will enact the greatest massacre in human history.

The cab draws up outside St Augustine's Cathedral, a Gothic wedding cake of orange brick and blackened stone. The cabby opens the little trapdoor in the roof of the cab and calls down, 'This is it. Go straight in. Squalida's expecting you.'

Jasper gets out of the cab, climbs the

steps outside the cathedral and passes through the entrance – a gargoyled arch.

Inside the cathedral the divine has evidently given way to the profane. Wooden signs point the way to BURGLARY, BLACKMAIL, LARCENY (PETTY AND GRAND), ASSASSINATION, ABDUCTION and a bewildering catalogue of other misdeeds. The cathedral is busy, people hurry to and fro, but the atmosphere is one of calm efficiency. What was once the high altar has been made into a reception desk, illuminated in jewelled splendour by the daylight that passes through the stained-glass window behind it. Jasper advances on the desk, but before he can reach it he is intercepted by a stooped little man wearing a jacket with grimy cuffs and collar. The man's face is as round as a full moon and he has a squint that would knock a tom-cat off a garden wall. He touches Jasper's sleeve with ink-stained fingers. 'Good day, Mr Pepper,' he says. 'Follow me, if you please.'

Jasper is suspicious. 'How d'you know who I am?'

The little man laughs as he breathes in, and the result sounds as if something in him wants oiling. 'Miss MacHeath told me that a gentleman named Pepper would be calling on her. Since you're better dressed and cleaner than most of our clientele, I took the liberty of assuming that you were the said gentleman, sir.'

He leads Jasper across the cathedral, through a door, along a corridor and up a spiral staircase made of iron to the door of Squalida MacHeath's office, a room ingeniously constructed in the base of the cathedral's spire. The little man abandons Jasper and disappears below.

Jasper knocks at the door and a voice invites him to enter.

Here is Squalida MacHeath, wearing a dress that is a symphony of dove-grey silk.

She is reclining on a chaise longue, holding a letter that she took from a mailbag that stands nearby. Balls of scrunched-up paper are scattered hither and thither. Behind the chaise longue, a chocolate-point Burmese cat sleeps in a basket set on a plinth made from an old lectern. When Jasper comes in, Squalida crumples the letter in both hands, tosses it over her left shoulder, looks him boldly in the eye and says, 'You're a demonist.'

Jasper is startled by this abrupt start to the conversation, and is about to deliver his customary blustering denial when he remembers whom he is addressing. He draws off his hat in a sweeping bow and says, 'I am, Miss MacHeath.'

'You're better looking than the other demonists I've met,' says Squalida. 'They were a scrawny lot and barking mad. Are you mad, Mr Pepper?'

'Not as far as I'm aware,' Jasper says.

'Demonism will bring you to it in

the end. Always does,' says Squalida. 'Sit down.'

Jasper looks around and coughs in an embarrassed way. 'There doesn't seem to be a chair, Miss MacHeath.'

Squalida points downwards. 'See that carpet? It's Persian and it's worth hundreds. If the floor's good enough for the carpet, it's good enough for you.'

Jasper seats himself cross-legged.

'Supple too!' Squalida observes. 'Well?'

'Er . . . well?'

'Have you got it?' Squalida brisks.

At first Jasper is dumbfounded, for it appears that Squalida knows what she couldn't possibly know – unless . . .

'Febbo!' Jasper says quietly.

'Febbo indeed!' Squalida confirms. 'Dear Luigi sang like a mynah bird. It's a pity that he can't be with us, but he's been called away to Timbuktu on urgent business. He left early this morning and won't be back for ages. You haven't answered my question.'

Jasper, grasping that pretence is not only futile but dangerous, says, 'I don't have the sphinx but I know who does – my nephew, Crispin Rattle, aged twelve, lately of St Peter's Lane, London.'

Squalida shudders. 'Ugh, London!' she exclaims. 'A dreadful place! I got stuck on a train for an hour in London once. I almost lost the desire to go on living. Where is the boy now?'

'In Wolveston.'

'And more specifically?'

'I don't know his address,' Jasper says.

'Are you telling me the truth?' Squalida asks warily.

'Miss MacHeath, I'm neither a fool nor a brave man. I'm quite aware of what would happen to me if I dared to tell you anything *but* the truth.'

'What does your nephew look like?'

'I haven't the least idea,' Jasper says.

'May I ask you a question?'

'You may, but I may not answer it,' says Squalida.

'You don't strike me as being a dabbler in demonism, Miss MacHeath, so why are you interested in the sphinx?'

'Money,' Squalida replies honestly. 'Can you really use the sphinx to talk to the dead?'

'I'm convinced of it.'

'What if it's a fake?'

Jasper smiles mirthlessly. 'I shall be rather disappointed,' he says.

Squalida shifts a cushion to make herself more comfortable. 'Here's what I propose,' she says. 'I'll make all my resources available to you, and sooner or later we'll find your nephew and the sphinx. You'll use your knowledge of demonism to discover if the sphinx is genuine. If it's not, we'll sell it to the richest chump we can find and split the proceeds ninety–ten in my favour.'

'And if it is genuine?' enquires Jasper.

'We'll make a fortune!' Squalida sighs. 'Plenty of confidence-tricksters wangle themselves a fair living by setting up as mediums and pretending to pass on bogus messages from the Other Side. Think what people would pay for the real thing! It'll be tantamount to founding a new religion.'

Jasper finds the thought of sharing power and riches extremely offensive, but does not let it show. Hesitantly he says, 'Begging your pardon, Miss MacHeath, but you have so far put only one proposition to me. Am I to be offered an alternative?'

'Certainly!' says Squalida. 'The alternative is for you to be in a sack weighted with lead, at the bottom of the Bast.'

'Then I agree to your terms,' says Jasper.

You are a fool, Squalida MacHeath! he thinks. I shall use you to get what I want and I shall get rid of you as soon as it's convenient.

Coincidentally, Squalida is having the selfsame thoughts about Jasper.

An hour later, having been returned to the respectable quarters of the city, Jasper takes a turn along Broadway. He normally avoids the street, since too much contact with humanity nauseates him, but today his mood has turned decidedly expansive. Squalida MacHeath has volunteered herself as his useful puppet. Through her agency, Jasper will obtain the sphinx and then . . . and then . . .

Jasper ducks into a small café and takes a window seat. He orders a glass of white wine – a rare indulgence – and gazes idly through the window, lost in pleasant daydreams, until a building across the street distracts him from his reveries. It is a preposterous architectural mishmash that is intended to be Egyptian. Beside the door of the building is a large poster affixed to a billboard. One of the words on the poster stands out from the rest: CALLISTO.

'Callisto?' whispers Jasper. His eyebrows knit together as he tries to recall where he has come across the name before.

CHAPTER SEVENTEEN
A DEMONIST IN PARADISE LANE

When Callisto and Aril return to Scarlatti Mews after their performance on Monday evening, Crispin joins them at the supper table, but says very little. Callisto senses that Crispin is concerned about something, and tries to coax him by asking, 'How did you get on without us?'

'All right,' says Crispin. 'Mrs Moncrief told me about William Shakespeare – he was a bit of a lad, wasn't he?'

'The greatest dramatist these islands have yet produced, and far and away the most able cryptographer,' Callisto says. 'If he hadn't broken the Spanish Naval Code in 1588, the Armada might not have been defeated, and—' He breaks off as he marks the faraway look in Crispin's eyes. 'What's on your mind, Crispin?'

Crispin takes a bite from a gherkin. 'I been thinking about what that professor said this morning. It mixed me up and I'm trying to get it straight. Who does the sphinx really belong to?'

Callisto dabs at his lips with a napkin. 'Who indeed? It has been lost, bought, sold and stolen countless times over the centuries. There are many demonists who would pay a great deal of money to come by it, and they would use its powers to do great evil.'

Crispin is astonished at the notion of there being such persons as demonists, but before he can say anything, he is interrupted by an outburst from Aril.

'Almost as much evil as the sphinx will do to you if you keep it in this house!' she exclaims, slamming down her knife and fork. 'I can hardly breathe, it's so stuffy in here. I'm going into the garden for some fresh air.' She stands up and leaves the room.

'Is she sickening for something?' says Crispin.

'It's the week of the full moon,' Callisto says absently. 'Aril may have to go away for a day or so.'

'Go away where?' says Crispin.

Callisto ignores the enquiry. 'I'll try to explain about the sphinx as straightforwardly as I can, but it's a complicated matter,' he says. 'If I begin to bore you, you must tell me at once – agreed?'

'Agreed,' says Crispin.

Callisto takes a groat from his pocket and turns it to show Crispin, first the profile of Lord Protector Groves, and then the snarling face of the British Dragon. 'Another world runs parallel to the world we know, the way that the Lord Protector and the dragon are on opposite sides of this coin,' he says. 'Though each world depends for its existence on the other, contact between the two is virtually, but not entirely, impossible. The sphinx makes contact easier.'

'Has this other world got a name?' says Crispin.

'Many names, some of which are perilous to say aloud,' Callisto says. 'The most harmless name is Inferno.'

Shock and perplexity cross Crispin's face in rapid succession. He giggles nervously. 'Cor, you had me going for a minute there, Mr Callisto! I thought you was serious.'

'I'm deadly serious,' Callisto assures him.

'But angels and devils is all flimflam!' protests Crispin. 'It's just talk to keep the poor ignorant and the parsons rich.'

Callisto hears the voice of Rachel Pepper speaking through her son. 'There are many who would agree with you, Crispin, and I heartily wish that I was one of them, but unfortunately I can't be. In my life I've learned many things that I would rather not have known.'

'I don't want nothing to do with religion!' Crispin maintains stubbornly.

'And no one here will force you to have anything to do with it,' says Callisto. 'However, there are some who want to have everything to do with religion and who would do anything to own the sphinx.'

'Is that why my uncle got murdered?' says Crispin.

'I believe so.'

Crispin gulps. 'What we going to do with the sphinx then, Mr Callisto?'

'I haven't the faintest notion,' Callisto says. 'In the eyes of the law it should go back to the Russian museum from which it was taken, but if it was stolen from there once it could be stolen again. Besides, there is also the problem of how to return it. One could hardly send such an object via the mail.'

Crispin gets to his feet. 'I'll deliver it personal!' he announces. 'When's the next train to Russia?'

Callisto is impressed by Crispin's courage. The boy has only just discovered that his uncle was murdered on account of the sphinx, and now wants to carry it by hand halfway across the world!

'I admire your spirit, Crispin, but matters can't be settled as straightforwardly as that,' says Callisto, consulting his pocket watch. 'Would you mind going into the garden and asking Aril to come inside? I'm worried that she'll catch a chill if she stays out any longer.'

It is a clear night. Aril is standing motionless on the back lawn, staring into the sky. Serene though she seems, as he draws closer Crispin senses that she is restless. Beneath her outer calm, something is fizzing away like sherbet.

'What you doing?' says Crispin.

'Looking at the moon,' Aril says.

Crispin does likewise. 'Bright, ain't it?' he says. 'Shining like a shilling on a sweep's backside.'

'My people call the moon "The Seeker",' says Aril. 'She calls to her lost children as she searches the night for them. Listen!'

'Can't hear nothing,' Crispin says.

'You can if you listen with your blood,' says Aril.

Crispin peers at her. Her face looks different in the moonlight, fierce and imperious.

'Aril, was you a princess back in your own country?' Crispin says.

'My people have no princes or princesses,' says Aril.

'Yeah, but you got maharajas and that, ain't you?'

'The Indians do,' says Aril. 'My people are not Indian.'

Crispin is confused. 'But I thought you was from India.'

'I am,' says Aril, 'but where you're from isn't who you are. My people have no country. Their only home lies in themselves.' The irises of Aril's eyes turn golden, and the colour swirls. Her voice is low and husky as she says, 'I can feel it wanting us. It has hunted us for thousands of years, and now—'

'Turn it up, Aril!' pleads Crispin. 'You'll have me in a funk if you're not careful.'

Aril smiles and is herself again. The princess of the night has gone. 'I'm sorry,' she says. 'Shall we go in and ask Mrs Moncrief to make us some cocoa?'

It is Tuesday night in Scarlatti Mews. Callisto and Aril are performing at the theatre. Crispin and Mrs Moncrief are seated either side of the fireplace in the parlour, in companionable silence. Mrs Moncrief's needles quietly click as she knits a blue- and pink-striped tea cosy. Crispin stares at the faces, mountains and castles in the glowing heart of the fire. Since he met Callisto, Crispin's days have been a wonder and a whirl, and he is glad of this quiet time when he can sit and think his own thoughts.

Suddenly the clattering of hooves on cobbles sounds outside, and shortly afterwards there is an urgent rapping at the door.

'Who can that be, so late?' Mrs Moncrief says with a frown.

'Shall I go, ma'am?' offers Crispin.

Mrs Moncrief tilts back her head and peers down her nose at Crispin. 'I'm sure I know my duties as a housekeeper, thank you, Crispin Rattle,' she says pertly.

Mrs Moncrief answers the front door. Crispin hears muffled voices, an exclamation, then Mrs Moncrief returns. Her face displays no emotion, but she has been so badly shaken that she forgets to project her voice, and speaks normally as she says, 'They have sent a cab from the theatre. There has been an accident. Miss Aril has been injured and is asking for you. We must go to her at once.'

Crispin is already in the hall. Through the opened door he sees the waiting cab. The driver resembles a monkey. Crispin grabs his cap and overcoat and steps outside while Mrs Moncrief extricates her umbrella.

Strong arms seize Crispin. A hand holding a cloth is clamped over his nose and mouth. He breathes in heady fumes.

A rising tide of night sweeps through him. Waves roll in: fast, and black, and overwhelming.

Callisto has not been himself for days. His performances at the Egyptian Hall have been as deft as ever, but have lacked a little of their customary sparkle.

Aril has, with difficulty, restrained herself from commenting on Callisto's preoccupation, but as they leave the stage door and step into Paradise Lane, she can bear his lack of attention no more. She brings him to a halt by standing directly in front of him and saying, 'Come back!'

'Back?' says Callisto.

Aril lifts her hand and touches his forehead. 'From in there,' she says. 'Talk to me!'

Callisto sighs loudly. 'It's that wretched sphinx,' he confesses. 'I can't make up my mind about it.'

'No, it's the sphinx that's keeping you from making up your mind,' Aril says. 'I can feel it working on you. The longer you put off your decision, the tighter its hold on you will be.'

Callisto sees the truth in this. The sphinx has occupied his thoughts every waking hour. 'You're right, Aril!' he says. 'Tomorrow morning, I'll—'

Jasper Pepper steps out of the shadow into a circle of lamplight. Beneath his bloodshot eyes, his face is wrapped in a black silk scarf. 'I want the Black Sphinx,' he says.

'Stay back!' snaps Callisto, holding out his hand. 'Are you deranged, man?'

'I want the Black Sphinx!' Jasper insists.

'And I want to be left in peace,' says Callisto. 'You must have mistaken me for someone else, for I don't know what you're talking about.'

'We have the boy,' Jasper says. He reaches inside his coat and produces Crispin's cap.

Aril gasps.

'He is quite safe,' Jasper continues, 'but he won't stay safe if you don't hand over the Black Sphinx.'

'You, sir, are a cowardly blackguard to threaten the life of a young boy!' seethes Callisto.

'It will be a long while before his life is threatened, but it will be a long while that he will not enjoy,' Jasper says. 'He may lose some fingernails, or perhaps an ear, if you are not prompt.'

Callisto clenches his fists and steps forward.

'Come, come, none of that!' Jasper chides. 'If you assault me, or attempt to hold me hostage, the boy will be harmed.'

'Calm down, Callisto,' Aril says gently.

'The young lady is right,' says Jasper. 'Calm down and listen. You are to bring the sphinx to St Augustine's in Gospelmaker Road. If you are not there by midnight, the boy will suffer.'

'St Augustine's?' Callisto says. 'Is Squalida MacHeath mixed up in this?'

'Miss MacHeath has all sorts of fingers in all sorts of pies,' says Jasper. 'But time is wasting, and I must bid you adieu. I advise you to make haste. Unpunctuality would have the gravest consequences.' He sidles back into the shadows and slopes off towards Broadway.

'Damnation!' curses Callisto. 'If only I

had acted sooner! If only I had taken more care!'

'That man is a demonist,' says Aril. 'I smelled it on him.'

Her voice has a dreamily detached tone that Callisto recognizes. 'The moon is full?' he says.

Aril nods.

'Can you hold back until—?'

'I'll do what has to be done, Callisto,' says Aril. 'That man mustn't have the sphinx and Crispin must be rescued. Should we inform the police?'

Callisto laughs grimly. 'The police will not dare to cross Squalida MacHeath. We'll have to settle this affair ourselves.'

Chapter Eighteen
Prisoners

Alone in his cab on the road back to St Augustine's, Jasper Pepper finds that he is not alone. The demon Bazimaal is suddenly with him, shaped like the young woman who rode with him on the Wheel. She is smoking a slim cheroot.

'Well, even you must allow that I handled Callisto pretty well,' says Jasper.

'And now you're scurrying off to report back to Squalida MacHeath, like a sneaky schoolboy informing on his classmates,' the young woman says scornfully. 'That meddling she-cat doesn't realize the sphinx's true value. She only thinks of the gold that she stands to make. I'm disappointed in you, Jasper. How can you bring yourself to have dealings with someone who is so vulgar?'

Jasper grunts. 'Because Squalida MacHeath holds, as they say, all the trump cards. I have no choice but to comply with her wishes.'

'So you're to stoop to blackmail?' the young woman says. 'Your nephew's life in exchange for the Black Sphinx. Tawdry, to be sure, but effective.'

'Not so tawdry, perhaps,' says Jasper. 'All partnerships and agreements are temporary. Once I have the sphinx I'll kill my nephew, Callisto, Squalida MacHeath, and whomsoever else takes my fancy.'

The light of a passing lamp sweeps across the young woman's face, revealing the earnestness of her expression. 'Tread carefully around Callisto, Jasper,' she advises. 'He is far more resourceful than you may suppose.'

'Ha! You sound as if you know him,' remarks Jasper.

'I do, in a manner of speaking,' the young woman says. 'I killed his mother and he has sworn to destroy me.'

'He's nothing but a tuppenny music-hall conjuror, with his cards and doves!' sneers Jasper. 'He'll come to rue the day when he bandied words with a *real* sorcerer.'

The young woman draws on her cheroot, and its glowing orange tip winks. She blows out smoke that curls itself into feathers, claws, fangs.

Jasper coughs and clears his throat. 'That's a filthy habit you've got there,' he says.

'Ooh, smoking isn't the half of it, Jasper!' exclaims the young woman. 'But, since you object . . .' She pops the cheroot into her mouth and swallows it. 'Where were we?' she says brightly. 'Ah yes, the sphinx! How long have you been searching for it?'

Jasper shrugs. 'Merely a lifetime. For

millennia it has been cloaked in rumours, hints and whispers – mostly unreliable. I have travelled the world to track it down, denying myself pleasures that other people take for granted. Such has been my dedication and devotion.'

'There must have been times when you doubted success.'

Jasper has never shown any reluctance when it comes to talking about himself, and now he does so with evident relish. 'Doubt is an affliction of lesser men,' he says. 'Those who are destined for greatness are able to rise above such pettiness. My certainty has always been absolute. The unswerving faith that I have placed in myself will shortly receive its just reward. When I wield the power of the sphinx, humans and demons will worship me as a god.'

The young woman sadly shakes her head. 'That will never be, Jasper. All the while that you were searching for the sphinx, you were becoming its prisoner. You will not be its master, but its slave. It has manipulated you as though you were a marionette. Your life has been wasted and you have denied yourself for nothing.'

Jasper laughs slyly. 'The kind of thing, of course, that I anticipated you would say,' he says. 'I know that you fear me, Bazimaal, and with good reason. I intend to treat you in a particularly inventive manner.'

The young woman watches the benighted city slide across the window of the cab, and makes no reply.

For the briefest moment Jasper is aware of something – a flitting shadow, the turn of a cog wheel, the snagging of a thread? It seems that every action he has ever taken, every word he has ever spoken, were not his own, but elements in a drama written by someone else.

The fancy lasts no longer than a glint of

light on a jewel. Jasper is master of himself and his future, and soon he will be master of the world.

Crispin regains consciousness while vomiting into a white enamel bowl. His forehead is being bathed with a cool, damp cloth. A voice as soothing as gravy murmurs, 'There, there! You'll feel as right as ninepence directly, you'll see. That's it, sonny-my-lad.'

Crispin is lying on a bed. His hands are tied behind his back. The light of a candle in a niche wavers over grey stone walls. Squalida MacHeath is seated beside the bed, her eyes brimming with tender concern. 'Have you done being sick?' she asks. 'Would you like some water?'

She holds a cup up to Crispin's lips and he takes two swallows from it. 'Where am I?' he demands. 'Is this a hospital? Where's Aril? Are you a nurse? Where's Mrs Moncrief?'

Squalida smiles winningly. 'What a deal

of questions! To answer them in no particular order – I don't know where Aril is. Mrs Moncrief is probably at Scarlatti Mews, nursing a nasty headache. You're in a cell in the crypt of St Augustine's Cathedral, and I'm not a nurse, I'm Squalida MacHeath.'

Crispin, remembering his manners, says, 'Pleased to meet you, miss.'

'Mutual, I'm sure,' says Squalida. It is obvious that Crispin has never heard of her, and she is delighted.

Crispin ignores his pulsing headache and slowly reasons out his situation. 'So Aril didn't have no accident then?'

'That was a strategic fib to lure you out of the house,' reveals Squalida. 'As far as I know, Aril is as fit as a squirrel. You, on the other hand, are a bit queasy, on account of the after-effects of spirits of ether.'

'Stap me, I've been nobbled!' Crispin cries. 'I'm a prisoner.'

'I prefer the term "compulsory guest",' says Squalida.

As Crispin's headache recedes, his wits sharpen. 'This is about that sphinx thing, ain't it?'

'Partly. Mostly it's about money,' Squalida frankly admits. 'I want you to behave yourself while you're here – which won't be long if everything goes according to plan. But if you make a fuss, or Callisto tries any funny business, I'll turn you over to your uncle.'

'My uncle?' whimpers Crispin.

'Mr Jasper Pepper,' Squalida says. 'He's a strange sort of a gentleman, not one that I would care to be turned over to, let me tell you. Mr Pepper holds some peculiar beliefs, and I don't think that nephews rank highly on his list of earthly blessings.'

Crispin feels the touch of a fear that threatens to turn into a grip. 'I reckon you're backing a loser, miss,' he says. 'Mr Callisto won't ever give up the sphinx for me.' He tries a wink and a wry smile. 'You don't seem a bad sort to me, miss. How's about turning me loose, eh?'

Squalida's laughter resounds throughout the cell. 'Oh, you've got charm, all right, I'll grant you that!' she gurgles. 'You'll break a few hearts when you're older, if you live to be older.' Her merriment evaporates, her expression hardens. Crispin glimpses the steel that lies beneath the satin and lace.

'Although I might not seem a bad sort, I'm thoroughly bad,' says Squalida. 'There's no point in trying to appeal to my better nature, for I haven't one.' She points to the candle. 'Your life means no more to me than that. While you're useful to me, I'll keep you burning, but once you're not—' She leans forward and puffs air into Crispin's face. 'Understand?'

'Gotcha,' says Crispin.

Squalida rises from her chair. 'Make yourself comfortable. There's a man standing guard outside. Call him if you need anything.' She crosses to the door and raps it with her knuckles. The door opens, Squalida steps through and the door closes with a clang.

Crispin stares at the dark ceiling and tries to make his mind a blank; he fears that if he thinks, he will lose himself in panic.

CHAPTER NINETEEN
IN THE CRYPT

The cab proceeds so slowly, Aril thinks, that it is as if the road has been coated with molasses. She turns to say something to Callisto, but decides against it. His expression is grim. A muscle in his jaw bunches and relaxes, bunches and relaxes. He is icy with anger, as furious as a blizzard. Aril has seen him like this before, and normally his mood would alarm her, but this is not a normal night and something wild in her revels in his rage.

Aril can see the full moon in the sky overhead, can see where it bathes the roofs of Wolveston in silver. The shadowy craters on the moon's face make a shape that resembles a crouching hare. The hare is a worthy adversary, cunning, nimble and speedy. The joy of the hunt begins to course through Aril's body.

The cab careers along Eden Road into Pinchbeck Street, and so to Scarlatti Mews. Callisto and Aril get out. 'Wait here,' Callisto instructs the cabby.

The cabby touches the brim of his bowler. 'Right you are, sir!'

Within Scarlatti Mews waits the indomitable Mrs Moncrief, after whose health Callisto anxiously enquires.

'I have been waylaid and etherized by thugs, but having fortified myself with smelling-salts and liquorice water, I am equal to anything,' says Mrs Moncrief. 'Tell me about Crispin.'

Callisto tells her, and as his account goes on, Mrs Moncrief scowls, and grinds her teeth.

'So Aril and I must take the sphinx to St Augustine's,' Callisto concludes.

'And I will accompany you,' says Mrs Moncrief. 'I cannot stay idle here while Crispin is in peril, and the insult I have suffered this evening cannot go unanswered. Squalida MacHeath will learn that it does not pay to trifle with Letitia Moncrief!' She leans in close to Callisto and whispers, 'It's a full moon tonight. Is Miss Aril—?'

'Aril will be as we need her to be,' Callisto says. 'The plan I've devised depends upon surprise, and I think you'll agree that there is no surprise more surprising than Aril.'

The sphinx, still in its leather grip, is brought out of its place of concealment in Callisto's wardrobe, and all seems ready. However, just when Aril, Mrs Moncrief and Callisto are about to mount into the cab, a hitch presents itself in the form of the cabby.

'St Augustine's, please,' says Callisto.

The cabby's jaw drops until his face is almost as long as his horse's. 'No fear, sir!'

he exclaims. 'I'm not going into the Scarp at this time of night.'

'Not for ten dragons?' says Callisto.

'You can offer me what you like, sir. I won't go into the Scarp for love nor money,' the cabby says stubbornly.

Mrs Moncrief points her umbrella at the cabby in an accusing manner. 'Then climb down and make way for someone who will!' she says.

'Hey?' says the cabby. 'You can't drive my cab, lady. You haven't got a licence.'

'That's just where you are wrong, my man!' Mrs Moncrief says triumphantly. In one gliding movement she reaches into the pocket of her coat and brings out a pewter badge inscribed,

WOLVESTON GREATER CIVIC COUNCIL
CAB DRIVER LICENCE 14287
MONCRIEF L. (MRS)

'I qualified thirty years ago so that I might earn a crust at times when my talents as an actress were not in demand,' says Mrs Moncrief, holding the badge up to the light of a nearby lamp so that the cabby can read it. 'Alas, they were never in demand, but I kept my licence anyway!'

'But—!' is the only protest the cabby is allowed, for Mrs Moncrief clambers up to the driver's seat and shoves him aside with a swing of her hips.

The cabby tumbles down and stands perplexed on the cobbles. 'My cab!' he protests. 'How can I make a livelihood without a cab?'

Callisto presses a ten-dragon piece into the cabby's hand. 'Come back tomorrow. If your cab isn't here, it will be at St Augustine's.'

The cabby is partly appeased by this. Indeed, considering how few customers there generally are at this hour, he has probably turned a profit. 'All right, sir,' he says. 'But if you play me false, you'll hear from my brief.'

Mrs Moncrief places two fingers in her mouth, whistles shrilly, and the cab horse breaks into a canter. Then the peerless housekeeper opens the trapdoor in the roof and bends her head down so that she can listen to Callisto as he outlines his plan.

Aril listens too. The pupils of her eyes are changing shape from circles into pointed slits.

There are two guards on night duty outside the doors of St Augustine's Cathedral. Their names are Mr Lipman and Mr Sparks, and they are a cut above the usual sort of ruffian to be found in the Scarp. They look very much alike, though Mr Lipman is a shade the taller of the two. Both have blond hair, blue eyes, white eyelashes and athletic frames. Both wear charcoal-grey pinstriped three-piece suits which were tailored by Everett Row's finest, and which fit immaculately.

Mr Lipman and Mr Sparks have been inseparable companions since the day they met as junior masters at St Bardulph's Academy for Young Gentlemen of Quality, in Oxford. The road that leads from the world of private education to the world of crime is long and circuitous, and Mr Lipman and Mr Sparks have left no bend or fork in that road unexplored.

'Where has Waller got to, Mr Sparks?' asks Mr Lipman. 'I was under the impression that he was supposed to be on duty with us tonight.'

'He is in the crypt, Mr Lipman, keeping watch over a detainee,' Mr Sparks says.

'And who might that detainee be, Mr Lipman?'

'I couldn't tell you, Mr Sparks,' says Mr Lipman, 'but I've an inkling that the gentleman we saw just now has something to do with it.'

'Him?' Mr Sparks says disapprovingly. 'I found him puzzling, Mr Lipman. He was careless of his appearance – lovely clothes, but in such urgent need of sponging and pressing.'

'Careless of his personal hygiene too,' adds Mr Lipman. 'I estimate that he has been a stranger to his bath for upwards of a week. If I should ever turn that way, shoot me dead at once, would you, Mr Sparks?'

'A pleasure, Mr Lipman.'

The grinding of cab wheels, a sound not often heard in the Scarp after dark, distracts the guards. Simultaneously they turn their heads in time to witness a remarkable sight. A skinny beldame is driving a hansom cab at a brisk lick down Gospelmaker Road. She grips the horse's reins in her right hand, while her left hand wields a large black umbrella.

'Now there's something you don't see every day, Mr Sparks,' says Mr Lipman.

'Indeed not,' Mr Sparks concurs. 'But do you really think that the old biddy is a cabby? She looks more like a housekeeper to me.'

Before Mr Lipman is able to express an opinion, the cab pulls up beside the cathedral and two people spill out onto the pavement. One is a serious-faced man who wears a black cloak and carries a leather grip. The other is a lithe, dark-skinned girl with extraordinary eyes. The man and the girl mount the cathedral steps.

Mr Lipman and Mr Sparks square their shoulders.

'What's your business here?' says Mr Lipman.

'I've a special delivery for Miss Mac-Heath,' the man says.

'Leave it with us. We'll make sure that she gets it,' says Mr Sparks.

'I would rather deliver it in person, if you don't mind,' the man says.

'I wouldn't mind in the least, but would Miss MacHeath mind?' says Mr Sparks.

Mr Lipman looks the man up and down and speculates: forty(ish), well-dressed, well-groomed, presentable. Could be Squalida's new fancy man, thinks Mr Lipman.

'What's your name?' he says.

'Callisto.'

'And the young lady?'

Callisto looks mystified. 'Young lady? What young lady?'

'The young lady standing there beside you,' says Mr Lipman.

Callisto stares hard into Mr Lipman's eyes and says, 'You can't see any young lady with me.' He turns to Mr Sparks. 'And nor can you.'

'Young lady?' says Mr Sparks. 'What young lady? I didn't say anything about a young lady. Did you, Mr Lipman?'

'I didn't, Mr Sparks,' says Mr Lipman. 'If you'll step this way, Mr Callisto. I'm sure you don't want to keep Miss MacHeath waiting.'

Callisto signals to Mrs Moncrief to stay with the cab, then follows Mr Lipman inside, and Aril follows Callisto. Once inside the cathedral, she slips behind a thick stone pillar and breathes in deeply through her nostrils. She smells the musty odour of stale sanctity, and the unmistakable scent of Crispin Rattle. The scent is like a thread in the air. Aril lets the thread draw her on.

Down in the crypt of St Augustine's, Waller Dolman, the guard posted outside Crispin's cell, is feeling ill-used. Waller enjoys the company of others, particularly when ale-drinking and brawling are involved, and his solitary condition means that he only has himself to converse with to pass the time.

'A grown man standing watch over a nipper!' he grumbles. 'A waste of resources, that's what it is. This is what comes of letting a woman wear the trousers.'

As if the burden of his loneliness were not enough to bear, Waller has never found the crypt a congenial spot. It is lit by candles that cast shifting shadows, producing an eerie effect which stimulates Waller's customarily dormant imagination. He has strange fantasies concerning torture chambers and headless monks. The slightest noise makes his skin twitch, and the crypt is a plentiful source of slight noises, from creaks like the opening of coffin lids, to a perpetual bubbling that puts him in mind of a cauldron of slime coming to the boil. So when Waller hears a louder noise, a hoarse breathing and a death-rattle growl, his hand goes down to his belt and immediately draws his sheath knife.

The growl deepens. A shadow steals across the wall of the spiral staircase, and a figure appears.

Waller is dumbfounded. He appears to be confronted by a person done up for a fancy-dress ball. The figure has a human posture and wears human clothes, but the rest is sheer pantomime. Those long, pointed ears, that muzzle and those fangs must be made of rubber; the coarse and grizzled fur has surely been stuck on with spirit gum, and the black claws moulded from papier-mâché. The creature's appearance is almost comic, which renders it wholly terrifying.

Fear, like an elixir of youth, makes Waller a child again. 'Keep off me, bogey-man!' he shouts, holding up the knife.

The sight of the blade provokes the beast's fury. With a savage snarl it bounds at Waller, and delivers a backhanded slap to his face that lifts him clean off his feet and slams him into the wall. His head strikes stone, and he collapses into seething red darkness.

Inside the cell, Crispin steels himself. He has heard the shouting but does not know what it signifies. As he tries to sit upright, the door of the cell explodes inwards with a deafening thump. Fragments and splinters of wood radiate out like shrapnel. A bolt, bent out of recognition, clatters across the floor and a monster enters.

Crispin is convinced that his last moment has come, and that this dreadful creature is death incarnate. But though he is more afraid than he knew he could be afraid, he cannot take his eyes off the thing. It fascinates him as a cobra fascinates a rat.

The beast lurches across the cell. Its fur shrinks into its skin, its claws, fangs, ears and muzzle recede, and Aril stands before Crispin. Her shoulders are stooped, her face is lowered. 'You know my secret now, Crispin Rattle,' she says. 'You know my shame. Demon blood runs through my veins. You won't want to be my friend any more.'

Crispin cannot explain what he has just witnessed, nor is he sure that he desires an explanation, but two simple facts are clear: Aril is with him, and he is overjoyed to see her. 'Not want to be your friend?' he hoots. 'Don't be daft! Untie me and let's get out of here.'

Aril's fingers pick at the knots of Crispin's bonds. 'Mrs Moncrief is waiting outside with a cab,' she tells him. 'As soon as we join her, I'm to send Callisto a signal to let him know that you're safe, and then we're to go straight home.'

A voice says, 'I think, perhaps, not yet!' and Jasper Pepper steps into the cell. He is holding a double-action revolver.

CHAPTER TWENTY
IN THE LAND OF THE DEAD

Mr Lipman accompanies Callisto up to Squalida MacHeath's room and knocks on the door.

'Enter!' comes the reply.

Mr Lipman opens the door, ushers Callisto inside and says, 'Mr Callisto, Miss MacHeath.'

Squalida MacHeath is seated on her chaise longue, wearing a white lace negligée over which she has drawn a black satin peignoir. Her hair is artfully tousled and tumbles about her shoulders. Stretched across her lap is her Burmese cat; its eyes are closed and its purring is loud. An occasional table stands within easy reach of the chaise longue. On the table are two glass flutes and an ice bucket, from which protrudes the neck of a champagne bottle.

Squalida looks hard and long at Callisto, and the faint flush that appears on her cheeks indicate her approval of what she sees. 'Thank you, Mr Lipman, you may leave us,' she says.

Mr Lipman repeats his bow and closes the door.

Callisto glances round. 'Where is the demonist who brought me your summons?' he says.

'Jasper Pepper?'

Callisto flinches at the name and several puzzles resolve themselves in his mind.

'He's about somewhere,' Squalida says carelessly. 'He burbled something about lustral rites. Are you a believer in demonism, Mr Callisto?'

'My beliefs are neither here nor there, Miss MacHeath,' says Callisto. 'Shall we dispense with small talk and proceed directly to business?'

Squalida's pout is soft red prettiness. 'Business is so dry all on its own, don't you find, Mr Callisto? Come sit beside me and take a glass of champagne.'

Callisto is quite aware that he is being flirted with, and the current of attraction that flows between himself and Squalida MacHeath is by no means one-sided, but he needs to keep a clear head. 'Another time, perhaps,' he says.

'There's no time like the present,' Squalida murmurs wistfully.

Callisto places the grip on the table. His movement disturbs the Burmese cat, which jumps off Squalida's lap and scoots away.

'Here is the object you required me to bring,' says Callisto. 'No doubt you would like to inspect it.'

Squalida sighs. 'To be perfectly frank with you, Mr Callisto, this whole affair has begun to bore me. I don't take pleasure in abducting children, particularly when I abduct them at the behest of a mad demonist.'

'Is Jasper Pepper mad?' enquires Callisto.

'He's as mad as a mackerel,' says Squalida. 'I only need him to tell me that the sphinx is genuine. After he's done that, I'll have him done in.'

'Listen to me, Miss MacHeath,' Callisto pleads. 'The sphinx is highly dangerous. If it is used improperly, who knows what chaos and suffering will ensue? I implore you to release Crispin Rattle, and let me take the sphinx somewhere it may be safely disposed of.'

Squalida mimes a yawn. 'I like it better when you give me the glad eye,' she says. 'When you're being sincere, you sound like a bishop with a boil on his behind. I'll let the boy go for the sphinx. I'll let the sphinx go to the first one who offers me half a million in gold.'

'You're making a grave mistake,' says Callisto.

'Nothing that makes me money is a mistake, Mr Callisto.'

Callisto grows increasingly concerned. He estimates that he should have heard Aril's signal – a howl – by now.

Squalida notices Callisto's unease. 'Is something wrong?' she says.

Callisto laughs. 'It is night, I am alone in a room with the most notorious woman in Wolveston, and she asks me if something is wrong!'

'Only the most notorious woman in Wolveston?' Squalida says coyly. She looks to her right as she hears a knock at the door. 'Come in, Mr Pepper!' she calls.

And Jasper Pepper does come in, preceded by Aril and Crispin. Crispin's hands have been untied but he is far from free, for the muzzle of Jasper's pistol is pressed firmly against the side of his head.

'What's this?' cries Squalida.

'This is an escape attempt that I have foiled,' says Jasper. 'This boy is, as you know, my brat of a nephew. This girl is an abomination and I intend to burn her at the stake at the earliest possible opportunity. Where is the sphinx?'

'Here, in this bag,' Callisto says.

'Give it to me, or I will shoot the boy.'

'Don't, Callisto!' says Aril.

'Enough of this!' growls Squalida MacHeath. 'Mr Pepper, put down that gun and we will continue our negotiations like civilized people.'

Jasper's red-rimmed eyes glow with a fanatical brightness. 'But I am not a civilized person!' he snaps. 'I am a pagan and a demonist. Where there is order, I desire mayhem. Where there is harmony, I desire discord. Where there is peace, I desire conflict.' He looks at Aril. 'You, half-breed, place that bag at my feet.'

Aril's eyes meet Callisto's; he nods. Aril picks up the grip and puts it on the floor.

Jasper's spiritual vision shows him a crimson light dancing like fire around the grip. 'I feel the power of Imhotep!' he crows, and chants a few words in a guttural language.

Scarlet sparks radiate from the grip, humming and crackling as they seethe like grasping tentacles. The sparks dart outwards to strike at everyone in the room.

Like Jasper Pepper, Callisto can also feel power – his own power, draining out of him until he feels as wan as the flame of a match struck in full sunshine.

The walls become transparent, and Squalida MacHeath's room transforms into somewhere else.

Callisto, Avril, Crispin, Squalida and Jasper are now on the bank of a broad canal whose murky green water is motionless. In one direction the canal runs ruler-straight across a trackless desert of undulating sand dunes. In the other direction the canal disappears into the base of a gigantic pyramid built of black marble blocks.

The sky is white; the air is hot and dry.

Jasper peers in astonishment at his surroundings and his companions. The grip is still at his feet, the pistol is still in his hand; the rest is uncertain.

'Where the deuce is this place?' he splutters. 'Why are you people with me?'

No one knows the answer, and a heavy silence falls.

The silence is broken by the sound of someone whistling, and a gentleman appears on the crest of the nearest dune. His opera hat shows first, then his whiskered face, then his fur-collared overcoat. As he descends the dune and reaches level ground, the gentleman leaves off whistling to talk to himself and laugh.

'Well now!' he says. 'What's this, what's this? Who would have thought it, eh?'

'Malachi?' gasps Jasper.

And so it is: Malachi Pepper, wearing

the same clothes as when Jasper last saw him, in a rowing boat on the Bast.

'But I killed you!' says Jasper.

Malachi comes to a halt four metres from his brother.

'Oh, you killed me well,' he admits, 'and now I'm deader than custard.'

'I'll just make sure of that,' murmurs Jasper. He points his revolver at Malachi and squeezes the trigger.

But before the crack of the weapon's discharge reaches Jasper's ears, Malachi gives his body a limber twist, catches the bullet in his teeth and spits it onto the sand.

'Come, come, Jasper!' he says. 'That gun of yours won't do you any good here, you know.'

Callisto steps forward and bows politely.

'Forgive my intruding, but where is *here* exactly?' he asks.

'Why, the Land of the Dead,' says Malachi.

Squalida MacHeath titters somewhat hysterically.

'Which is the quickest way back to my crib in Wolveston?' she says.

'I'm afraid there is no going back, Miss MacHeath, only going through,' Malachi informs her.

Jasper's face is red with outrage.

'But I don't want to be in the Land of the Dead!' he exclaims, stamping his foot like a brat in the throes of a tantrum. 'I commanded the sphinx to transport me to the threshold of Inferno.'

'Then the sphinx appears to have disobeyed you,' Malachi remarks.

'Impossible!' barks Jasper. 'I have bound it to my will and it must do my bidding.'

'Perhaps it didn't hear you clearly,' Malachi suggests. 'Why don't you get it out of the bag and try again?'

Jasper stoops, and reaches down with his left hand, then recoils as red fire crackles from the open mouth of the grip. The fire

branches into a shimmering bush of ruby
flame.

'The sphinx is stronger here than in your
world, Jasper,' warns Malachi. 'It brought
you here to put you on trial. Each one
of you will be tested.'

He looks from Jasper to Callisto, to
Squalida, to Aril and finally to Crispin.

'Ah, you must be my nephew,' Malachi
says. 'You have your mother's eyes.'

'No I ain't!' protests Crispin. 'I've got eyes
of my own.'

And they see with exceptional clarity,
almost straight through Malachi to who
lies within him, and Crispin has a hunch
that it is the same person he has been
seeing in his mother's ghost.

Squalida pats her hair and trifles with a
ruffle on her peignoir.

'I can't be doing with trials of any kind,
I'm afraid,' she says. 'How much would it
cost to spring me out of this dump?'

'You can't bribe anyone in this world,'

Malachi says solemnly. 'Nor can you hire slippery lawyers to defend you. You must think for yourself, as all of you must.'

He raises his right arm and points.

'Go to the pyramid,' he says, and fades away; the fire bush above the grip vanishes along with him.

Jasper falls to his knees and clasps the grip to him.

'Just what the hell is going on?' wails Squalida.

'It would take too long to explain,' Callisto says, 'but I suspect that this world is subject to rules we had better abide by. Shall we . . . ?'

He offers his arm to Squalida and she takes it.

'Delighted, I'm sure,' she says.

In a like manner Crispin offers his arm to Aril, and he is thrilled when she accepts it.

Jasper gazes up at them. There is bafflement in his eyes.

'What are you doing?' he says.

'We're doing as we were told,' replies Callisto. 'We're going to the pyramid.'

Jasper clambers to his feet.

'I will lead the way,' he declares. 'Follow me!'

Callisto shakes his head in grudging admiration of Jasper Pepper: even in the Land of the Dead, the demonist's vanity knows no bounds.

CHAPTER TWENTY-ONE
THE RIDDLE AT THE
PYRAMID

Throughout her life, Squalida MacHeath has adhered to the principle that the world is real and is filled with a variety of useful solid objects – such as bullion bars and stiletto daggers – and not even the evidence she is currently receiving from her senses can shake her beliefs. She gives Callisto's arm a squeeze with her own, inclines her head closer to his and murmurs, 'This is your doing, isn't it? You've hypnotized me with your conjuring skills, you wicked man!'

'My dear Miss MacHeath,' objects Callisto, 'nothing could be further from—'

'Don't bother to deny it,' Squalida says with a twinkling wink. 'I know when I've been had, and this time I've been had good and proper. You've put me in a trance, but don't make the mistake of thinking that you've won. The game's not over yet.'

'So I observe,' says Callisto.

Crispin Rattle, meanwhile, is proving a puzzle to himself. By rights, his sudden transportation to another world should have left him gibbering with fear, but it has not. His life has been so peculiar since his parents' deaths that one more peculiarity is neither here nor there. He is more concerned for Aril than himself.

'Don't you worry,' he tells her. 'Mr Callisto will soon get us out of this, and I'm right here to protect you.'

But Crispin does not have the vaguest idea of the sheer danger he may face.

Jasper Pepper, on the other hand, has nothing but vague ideas. The crack in his sanity has widened to a breach. Though the entire affair of the Black Sphinx has been, for him, a train of soured promises, he nonetheless maintains an irrational and foolhardy optimism.

'A hitch, a hiccup, the slightest of delays,' he mumbles. 'The fairest prize is hardest won. All things come to those who wait. An Englishman's home is his castle.'

The formidable heat draws up sand into whorls that writhe and shimmy like exotic dancers. Directly ahead, the pyramid looms, dour and sinister. Its polished stones reflect the desert, the sky and the insignificant dots of the approaching party.

At long and weary last Jasper and the others reach the spot where the canal enters the pyramid via a monumental sandstone gateway which has no gate. The gateway is festooned with hieroglyphs. Its lintel has been carved with the likenesses of outlandish creatures: human bodies

with the heads of lions, vultures, cuttle-fish. There is an unsettling liveliness about these monsters, as if at any minute a tongue might loll, or a beak clack, or a tentacle twitch.

Crispin's shoulders wriggle in a shudder.

'Cor, I wouldn't fancy meeting any of that lot up a dark alley!' he exclaims.

Aril, who is of entirely the opposite opinion, says nothing.

A cobbled path follows the canal into the pyramid. On this path is seated an elderly woman, none too clean, wearing robes as brown and coarse as sacking. Her hair is wild and yellowy-white. One of her eyes is brown, the other fogged, like the eyeball of a boiled fish. Around her stand a number of small clay pots, sealed with wax and parchment. She jerks a thumb over her shoulder to indicate the gateway.

'That's where your road lies,' she says, 'but first I must be paid the price of entry.'

The skin of her face is so sun-beaten and wizened that she is more like a talking nut than a human.

Jasper curls his lip.

'Out of my way, crone!' he growls. 'I am the master of the Black Sphinx.'

'Not yet you're not,' says the old woman. 'There's more to mastery than ownership. Pay me the entry price!'

Jasper produces his gun.

'Begone, before I blow out your brains!' he bellows.

The old woman crooks the little finger of her left hand, and Jasper is jerked into the air until his heels dangle two metres above the ground. He feels as if an invisible giant has seized him by the throat. His face is purple. His legs jerk. He cannot breathe. The pistol slips from his grasp, bounces on the cobbles and plops into the canal.

Although the prospect of standing idly by while Jasper Pepper is throttled is a tempting one, Squalida MacHeath is anxious to return to normality, and Jasper's shenanigans are not bringing her any closer to it.

'Don't take on so, Grandma!' she chides. 'My companion was too hasty, admittedly, but if you let him go we can talk terms.'

'You are challenging me?' says the old woman.

'You can put it that way if you like,' Squalida says.

The old woman straightens her little finger and Jasper crashes down.

'How much is the entrance price?' Squalida enquires.

The old woman smiles slyly.

'All you have, in a way,' she says.

Immediately Squalida has the beldame's measure. Squalida has negotiated with many a slippery customer, and senses that she is in the presence of a customer more slippery than most.

'In what kind of way, Grandma?' she says cautiously.

'It will cost you your wits,' says the old woman. 'I'll put a question to you, and you'll need your wits to answer it. Answer correctly and I'll let you pass.'

'And if the answer is incorrect?' says Callisto.

'Then your wits are forfeit to me and you'll all wander through the desert until you die.'

If the old woman were a cat, she would be purring.

The heap of dusty clothes that is Jasper Pepper croaks, 'Dump the old biddy in the canal and have done with her!'

'Have a care, Pepper,' Callisto advises. 'I suspect that this venerable lady may be more dangerous than she seems.'

The old woman's smile widens and somehow becomes more threatening.

'No I'm not,' she says. 'I'm exactly as dangerous as I seem.'

Squalida loses her patience. She did not enjoy her desert walk and is keen to avoid repeating it.

'Enough!' she snaps. 'If I'm to be turned into a lunatic, I want it to be sooner rather than later. Ask your question, Grandma.'

The old woman shuts her good eye, and recites in a voice that is thinner than a draught through a keyhole.

'Speck by speck I grow, sifting on sifting. I am tiny, but none can stand against me. Walls crumble, armies perish, kings fall. I swallow towns and cities whole, I swallow realms and empires, speck by speck. Who am I?'

Crispin frowns.

'What kind of question's that?' he asks Aril.

'A riddle,' she says.

Callisto believes that he knows the riddle's solution, but hesitates to say so in case he is wrong.

Squalida is radiantly confident, and

since – so far as she is concerned – this is only a hypnotic delusion, what she says does not really matter, wrong or right. She opens her arms wide and declares, 'The answer is obvious. You surround us. You are sand.'

The old woman opens up her eye and screeches out an unrecognizable oath. She shifts on her hunkers and glowers sulkily.

'Your wits are quick and the test is done,' she says to Squalida. 'Each of you must take one of my pots and drink what it contains.'

'Why?' asks Callisto.

'Because it is required,' replies the old woman.

'And what do the pots contain?' says Squalida.

The old woman smiles fondly and says, 'Darkness.'

Jasper Pepper stands, slaps his lapels, adjusts his cuffs and tries his best to look dignified.

'I am the greatest demonist the world has ever known,' he announces. 'I will drink no darkness, nor anything else that your filthy hands have touched.'

'Without the darkness in you, as soon as you step inside the pyramid your soul will shrivel and burn like hair,' says the old woman.

'I don't believe a word of it,' says Jasper, turning up his nose.

'Then you will die,' the old woman assures him.

Callisto decides that it is time to break the deadlock.

'Stop making such a fuss, Pepper!' he says.

He steps over to the old woman, picks up a pot and breaks the seal. Beneath it, something flows as slowly as syrup. The pot contains a ladleful of night sky, with minute points of light dusted across the black.

Callisto brings the pot to his lips and

drinks. He tastes the bitterness of past regrets and betrayals beyond remedy: the weak father he never took the trouble to get to know; his haughty mother, always hungry for more magic; what might have been with Rachel Pepper. His conscience pricks him and is weighted.

When Squalida MacHeath, Jasper Pepper and Aril drink, they are also reminded of their hidden dreads and secret shames.

But the darkness has a different effect on Crispin. He recalls that just recently he was an orphan with nothing and no one, and now he has found friends who care about him.

You're a lucky little beggar, Crispin Rattle, he thinks, apart from being whipped off to the Land of the Dead and having an uncle who's loopier than a crocheted shawl!

Jasper's conscience has been troubled, but his conscience is such a wretched and neglected thing that he is easily able to overcome it. He is not where he planned to be, it is true, and he has lost his pistol; but he still has the Black Sphinx. He hefts the grip.

'I'm off,' he says, and strides briskly towards the pyramid.

'Wait, Pepper!' calls Callisto.

But Jasper will not wait, and the shadowy mouth of the gateway swallows him.

Chapter Twenty-Two
In the Ancient Dark

Jasper pauses to allow his eyes to grow accustomed to the gloom. He makes out a line of torches burning in sockets fixed to the wall. The line stretches for as far as he can see. Between the torches is blackness.

Jasper breathes in deeply through his nose and smells spices, oils, unguents and an underlying stench of corruption, like the smell in a meat store on a hot summer's day. Water is dripping somewhere nearby, and the rhythm of the drip is regular and relentless. The air is cool enough to dry the sweat on Jasper's forehead, leaving his skin feeling taut.

The darkness around him is ancient,

older than the world he has come from; older than time. It is the dark of gods. Universes have been born out of it, and they will return to it after they die. There is power here in the pyramid, power so vast that if Jasper were to use his spirit sight, he would be blinded.

Jasper draws himself to his full height and declares in a loud, clear voice, 'I greet you, Lord Anubis, Keeper of the Gates of Death! I am Jasper Pepper, the master of the Black Sphinx. I summon you to appear before me and pay me homage!'

Stillness; silence; only the dripping water moves and makes a sound.

'I command you!' Jasper roars.

The dark ripples and the torches rearrange themselves. There is now a narrow passageway to Jasper's left, where before the wall was solid. Jasper interprets the appearance of the passageway as an invitation.

'That's more like it!' he says under his breath.

He ambles along the passageway, stopping every now and then to admire a particularly fine wall painting. At regular intervals, niches have been set into the walls. In the niches stand statues of gods: Isis and Osiris, hawk-headed Horus, Sobek, Ammon.

'Minor deities,' Jasper remarks in a bored voice. 'Irksome parasites. I'll soon lick them into line and show them what it means to be a god.'

His thoughts settle into familiar patterns, comforting fantasies of demon talons rending human flesh, and rotting corpses rising from their graves.

Shall my throne be of plain gold, or studded with gems? Jasper thinks. Shall I have the skulls of my enemies made into wine goblets? Shall I have tea served at half-past three instead of four o'clock?

These fancies are so delicious that Jasper

loses track of time until he realizes, with a start, that whereas he may not be lost, he has walked a considerable distance without appearing to arrive anywhere. Surely he has passed that statue of Horus before, and that painting of Isis resurrecting Osiris?

Jasper halts and looks behind him, takes a few experimental steps and halts again. The passageway is deceiving him by changing direction as he walks through it. The sharp corner of a turn to the left flips over to the right, or straightens itself, or winds round in a spiral. The paintings, statues and torches are part of a revolving loop that repeats itself continuously.

As he forges onwards, Jasper addresses the passageway as though it were a disobedient dog.

'What, sir? No you don't, sir! I won't have it. You'll go that way, not this. And now you'll go this way, not that!'

But the passageway refuses to come to heel.

Jasper's nerves are strained to the point where he is all temper and no temperance. He raises his fist above his head and shakes it.

'You're playing a jape on me, and it's not fair!' he rants. 'In the name of the Black Sphinx, I demand that you stop.'

Obligingly, the passageway expands into a circular chamber with three doorways. The walls are smooth, and glowing with gold leaf. The floor is a chequer-board of black and white tesserae.

Jasper spies a stone bench set against a wall, and lowers himself onto it with a grateful sigh. He needs to take a breather before whatever may come next.

It would be soothing to count the black squares on the floor, he thinks, and then thinks that the thought was not his own. But nevertheless, it *would* be soothing to count the black squares, so he begins.

'One, two, three,' he mutters, 'eight, seven, four ... Confound it, that can't be right! I'll start again. One, two, twenty, seventeen ...'

The numbers will not come in their correct order.

'I won't be foiled by a floor!' Jasper says to himself. 'Let's use our cunning, Jasper. Select a number at random. Sixteen thousand perhaps. Count down from sixteen thousand, and when there are no more black tiles, subtract the number remaining from the original number, and the result will be the number of—'

He breaks off as he hears a noise approaching the doorway directly in front of him. There is a shuffling scuttle, a skitter and a twittering, and a scarab beetle scampers into the chamber. The beetle is the size of a cab horse. Torchlight gleams on its iridescent blue-black carapace.

Jasper watches in dumb horror as the insect creeps closer and rears up on its hind legs. Its antennae brush scratchily against his face, feeling their way around his eyes, nose and lips. He can see the creature's jaws moving from side to side, drooling a viscous liquid over his clothes.

The test, thinks Jasper. That blind old baggage said that there would be a test, and this must be mine. I will bear it like a god!

He closes his eyes. Unexpectedly, a nursery song from his childhood occurs to him, and he sings it in a broken whisper.

'Pussy cat, pussy cat, where have you been?
I've been up to Wolveston to look at the queen.
Pussy cat, pussy cat, what did you there?
I cut off her head, and then—'

The scratching of the scarab's antennae ceases as a brilliant glare shines red through Jasper's eyelids.

263

* * *

Callisto sprints to the gateway and peers inside the pyramid. He is quickly joined by Squalida, Crispin and Aril.

'Wherever can Jasper have got to?' asks Squalida.

'Uncle Jasper?' Crispin cries. 'Are you there?'

The echoing reverberations of his voice shrink to silence.

Aril scans the dark with the sharper senses of her inner wolf.

'He's gone,' she says.

'Gone where?' says Crispin. 'He was here just now.'

Callisto stares intently dead ahead.

'I think that in this pyramid a minute may last a lifetime, and a lifetime may pass in a second,' he says. 'We must keep together. Whatever happens, whatever you may see or hear, do not go back. Keep walking forward – understand?'

The others nod.

'Very well,' Callisto says. 'I will go first, then Miss MacHeath, then Crispin. Aril will act as our rearguard. Be under no mis-apprehension, once we are through this gateway, we will be in the gravest danger. Be prepared for anything.'

They walk into the ancient dark.

Callisto sees the same line of torches that Jasper saw, smells the same smells, senses the same power. He begins to appreciate the awesome magic of the Black Sphinx, a magic strong enough to carry five people to the Halls of the Dead while they are still living; a magic that makes nonsense of every philosophy that humanity has devised.

Squalida sniggers – a strange sound in such a place.

'To tell you the truth, Mr Callisto, I'm partial to a bit of danger,' she confesses. 'Danger is the salt and vinegar that adds savour to the fish supper of life.'

'No sane person would welcome the

danger that lies here,' Callisto informs her. 'Our souls are in peril.'

'I've never been much of a one for souls and ceremonies, and men in robes like frocks,' muses Squalida. 'I like churches, on account of the silverware on their altars and the lead on their roofs, but a soul's something I haven't had to put a value on. What's the going rate for one?'

The darkness answers in the distant tones of Jasper Pepper, faintly shouting, '—it's not fair!'

Callisto freezes.

'Did you hear that, Aril?' he says.

There is no reply.

Callisto looks over his shoulder. He sees no sign of Aril or Crispin, and the gateway is no longer visible.

'It seems that you and I are alone again,' says Squalida. 'Pity I didn't bring that bottle of champagne with me.'

Callisto struggles to remain calm. He is gravely concerned for Aril and Crispin, but he has faith in his ward. She is intelligent and resourceful enough to meet most challenges.

'Let's go on,' he says.

There is no way for Callisto to estimate how long he and Squalida MacHeath spend trudging down the cobbled path beside the canal, but it is a tense and tedious time.

Then Squalida emits a little yelp of surprise and says, 'Look, a door!'

And indeed, there is a door, lit by a torch; a wooden door painted with the image of a winged eye.

Squalida approaches the door with her right hand extended.

'I wonder where it leads?' she says.

'I don't think that we should—' Callisto begins to say, but he is too late. The door is open and the pyramid is swept away by a wave of sunshine.

Callisto and Squalida are on a street that is lined with shops. Cabs and carts roll by; smartly dressed couples laugh and chatter as they saunter past; and in the background is the muted roar of a great city going about its daily business.

Squalida claps her hands beneath her chin and laughs aloud.

'It's Wolveston!' she exclaims. 'I know this street. I'm back! The trance is broken.'

Callisto also recognizes their location. They are in Vossiman Street, which lies just behind Everett Row, in the heart of Wolveston's tailoring district. The shops specialize in the sale of gentlemen's fashion accessories.

'Your trance can't be broken, Miss MacHeath, for you were never in one to begin with,' says Callisto, 'and though this would seem to be Vossiman Street, I don't believe for a moment that it is.'

'But it looks so real!' Squalida says.

'Unreality generally does,' says Callisto.

He glances at the window of the nearest shop, and sees a display of walking sticks and umbrellas. A sign announces

BOWSER'S CANES
A walk just isn't a walk without a Bowser!

The door of the shop opens and an assistant appears, grinning broadly. He is smartly turned out in a grey pinstriped suit and a gold brocade waistcoat. His pate is bald, his chin is long and his eyes are utterly vacant, like the windows of an unoccupied house.

'Please do come in, sir and madam,' says the assistant. 'You'll find that the shop is stocked with all manner of interesting items.'

Squalida waves dismissively.

'Thanks all the same,' she says, 'but neither of us needs a—'

'Ah, but you do!' interrupts the assistant. 'Of course you do – it's quite plain.'

Callisto smiles wryly.

'And it's quite plain to me that we have no choice,' he says.

The assistant bows his head and says,

'The customer is right, as always, sir.'

The interior of the shop is crammed with racks and stands of sticks, canes, umbrellas and parasols.

The assistant slips behind the counter, still wearing his grin.

'Sir and madam have the air of a couple who have recently returned from a journey to foreign parts,' he says. 'Would I be correct in that observation?'

'You would,' says Callisto.

'Then I am sure that this will fascinate you.'

The assistant clicks his fingers.

One of the sticks in the rack fixed to the base of the counter flexes, flows, falls to the floor and becomes a cobra that lifts its head, spreads its hood and hisses at Callisto and Squalida.

'An Aswan cobra, the deadliest of its kind,' says the assistant. 'After being bitten by it, the average man gives up the ghost within seven minutes.'

Callisto, not being the average man, has no intention of giving up his ghost or anyone else's. He seizes a cane from the nearest stand and holds it out at arm's length to keep the cobra at bay.

The cobra hisses more loudly.

'Have a care, sir,' advises the assistant. 'You're holding a Bowser's Life Preserver, and there is more to it than meets the eye. And speaking of eyes, I feel I ought to inform you that a full-grown Aswan cobra, such as the one you are facing, is capable of spitting its venom between six and seven metres.'

Callisto notices that the cane he is holding has an ivory top carved into a fox's head. Beneath the neck of the fox is a brass eye, whose purpose Callisto guesses in a flash. He presses the stub with his thumb, pulls at the cane with his left hand, and unsheathes a long, slender blade of shining steel.

'I'm obliged for the warning,' says Callisto.

He flicks his wrist, and the edge of the blade decapitates the cobra. The serpent's headless body knots and writhes.

'Er . . . Mr Callisto?' Squalida quails.

All over the shop, sticks are turning into snakes. They thud onto the floorboards. Their scaly skin rasps against the wood, their hissing fills the air.

'I think we should leave now, Miss MacHeath,' says Callisto.

'But we can't!' Squalida says. 'The door isn't there any more!'

'If you would care to step over to my side of the counter and abandon your companion to his fate, miss, I can provide you with a safe exit,' says the assistant.

Squalida wrinkles her nose scornfully.

'What, and miss all the fun?' she asks, then she seizes a conveniently placed cudgel and uses it to dash out a snake's brains.

The assistant addresses Callisto.

'Perhaps at this juncture, sir,' he suggests

discreetly, 'you should avail yourself of magic.'

And Callisto sees that this is his test.

'Magic should not be used lightly or selfishly,' he says. 'It should be employed sparingly, and only at the right time and in the right place. At present, the time is suitable but the place is decidedly not. Men do not cast spells in the Halls of the Dead.'

The intense brightness of the light that floods the shop dazzles him.

'Callisto!' Aril calls. 'Callisto!'

'I don't get it,' says Crispin. 'One minute they're there, then I blink and they ain't. D'you think there's a lot of open manholes round here, Aril?'

'There's a lot of something,' Aril says.

Crispin sighs.

'I wish there was a bit more room, so I could take your arm again and help you feel safer,' he says.

273

His wish is granted. The cobbles shift beneath his feet and the path widens until it would comfortably accommodate four persons standing side by side.

Crispin clutches Aril's arm.

'I don't like it here!' he says. 'What shall we do?'

'Callisto told us to keep on going, no matter what,' says Aril.

And so they keep on going.

'That test the old lady talked about,' Crispin says. 'What d'you reckon it'll be? I hope it's not like one of them written tests that schoolkids have to do. I never been to school. Ma taught me bits and bobs of reading and writing.'

'I learned from Callisto – with a little extra help from Mrs Moncrief,' confides Aril.

Crispin squirms with embarrassment.

'Would you be offended if I asked you something personal?' he enquires.

'I won't know until you've asked,' says Aril.

Crispin chooses his words with care. 'When you came to bust me out of that big church, and you was all strong and hairy, what did you feel like?'

'Moon-wild,' says Aril. 'Jungle-wild. It's like a rising tide inside me. Callisto taught me how to control myself, but the she-wolf is always there, especially on nights when the moon is full.'

'I'm glad,' Crispin says.

Aril is surprised. 'Glad?'

'About the she-wolf and that,' Crispin tries to explain. 'If it wasn't for her, you wouldn't be you, and I'm glad you are.'

'Thank you,' says Aril, for she suspects that there was a compliment amidst the tangle of Crispin's words.

Then she smells a foulness that makes her gag.

'Phwoar!' Crispin says. 'What's that ronk?'

Shadowy figures move through the dark.

Paws scrabble, nails click on stone, faces come out of the black and into the torchlight: monkey faces – baboon faces.

The baboons' features are distorted. The dry yellow skin over their cheeks has peeled back to reveal grey bone. Blue flames lick at the hollow sockets of their eyes.

'What's up with them?' gasps Crispin.

'They're dead,' Aril says.

Dead or not, the baboons have long, curved fangs. They lunge forward and their jaws snap shut like mantraps.

Crispin flinches back to avoid losing a hand.

The baboons form a circle; they hoot and jibber.

'The test!' Aril murmurs. 'This is a test of my courage.'

'What, you going hairy again so's you can rip 'em apart?' ventures Crispin.

'No,' Aril says. 'I won't change. I mustn't change!'

She quivers. The quiver goes through

her, over her, making her shape indistinct.

A baboon's fangs clack a centimetre from the tip of Crispin's nose. He would swear that the beasts are getting bigger.

Through gritted teeth, Aril mutters, 'If I change, I'll kill, and killing is wrong! Even killing the dead is wrong!'

Light bursts around her and Crispin in a soundless explosion, and when the light finally fades, the baboons have disappeared.

Crispin and Aril are in a round chamber with three doorways and golden walls. Jasper Pepper is there, and so are Callisto and Squalida MacHeath.

At the centre of the chamber stands a god.

CHAPTER TWENTY-THREE
THE KEEPER OF THE GATES

The god is close to four metres tall. He has the body of a broad-shouldered, muscular man, and the head of an enormous jackal whose pelt is as black as ebony. A length of green silk has been bound round his chest, and below it he wears a wrap of white and yellow cotton. His feet are bare. Gold bracelets circle his wrists and upper arms, and his emerald necklet glints in the light of the torches.

Crispin has never been in the presence of someone so intimidating. In a whisper that is partly a squeak he says, 'Who's this geezer?'

'Lord Anubis, the Keeper of the Gates of

Death,' Aril whispers back. 'He passes judgement on the souls who come before him and decides which ones are worthy enough to pass through the gates, into the Country of Bliss.'

This sounds an important sort of occupation to Crispin, and he stares even more respectfully at Anubis.

Jasper Pepper's gaze, however, is far from respectful. He is piqued and petulant as he rises from the stone bench to address the god.

'See here, Anubis, this simply isn't good enough!' he snaps. 'I came here in all good faith, expecting the hospitality due to someone of my status. But I have been insulted and ignored by you, and accosted by a particularly repellant arthropod. I want these other people killed directly, and afterwards I shall require refreshment, reparation and a humble apology.'

Anubis's voiceless reply thunders silently.

'Hold your tongue, maggot!'

Jasper is so enraged that spittle sprays from his lips as he splutters, 'How dare you speak to me in that manner, you cur-faced lackey! I am Jasper Pepper, master of the Black Sphinx and I demand obeisance from you.'

'Hold your tongue!' Anubis says again. 'Be still!'

Jasper's hand goes up to his mouth. He pokes out his tongue, grasps it between his fingers and stands as still as stone.

Anubis turns his amber-coloured eyes on Squalida MacHeath.

'I salute you, woman,' he says. 'Your test showed the quickness of your thought and the depth of your determination.'

Squalida is all of a flutter.

'Thank you for saying so, your lordship,' she bubbles. 'One does one's best.'

'I have looked into your heart,' continues Anubis. 'There is more tenderness in it, more concern for others than you pretend.'

Even gods may overstep the mark, and Squalida twitches her head and sniffs to show that she has been offended.

'Please don't say any more, your lordship,' she says tartly. 'I have a reputation to maintain.'

Anubis shifts his attention to Callisto.

'We have met before, have we not, unworthy one?'

'That is true, my lord,' admits Callisto. 'I beg forgiveness for disturbing you once more.'

Anubis bares his teeth in a savage smile.

'I sensed your power at our first meeting,' he says, 'but when your test came, you showed that your power was tempered by restraint, and you gained my admiration.'

'My lord does me too much honour,' says Callisto, bowing his head.

Anubis looks at Aril and his voice softens.

'You are welcome, Daughter of the Moon,' he says. 'Like me, you are a hunter, and a howler in the darkness. You have shown great strength, courage and control. You are both wise and beautiful.'

Aril's response is a speechless blush.

'And you have yet to be tested, heathen boy,' Anubis says to Crispin.

Crispin is afraid, but not too afraid to retort, 'I might not have much in the way of courage, strength, power or quick-thinking, but if I'm going to have a test, I reckon now's the time to give it me.'

Anubis points towards the leather grip beneath the bench where Jasper was seated.

'Bring me the Black Sphinx.'

Crispin shuffles his feet and mumbles, 'Begging your pardon and everything, but Mr Callisto told me as how I shouldn't ought to touch it.'

'Boy, you are the only one here who *can* touch it,' declares Anubis. 'For millennia the Black Sphinx has been handled by those whose souls were dark with greed, and hatred, and the lust for power. You are a spotless innocent. That is why, long before you were born, the sphinx chose you to deliver it to me.'

This is all beyond Crispin, and to tell the truth he feels somewhat let down. He had thought that his test would involve at least a tussle with something or other, but it turns out that he has to fetch and carry, like a porter at a railway station. He crosses the chamber, thinking, Blooming sphinx! It's turned my life clear upside down and I'll be glad to see the back of it.

He crouches, plunges his hands into the grip and lifts out the Black Sphinx.

'Place it before me,' says Anubis.

Crispin obeys, then steps back to Aril's side.

Anubis waves his arms in a ritual gesture.

A sudden gust of wind whistles through the chamber. The flames of the torches slant to one side, gutter and burn pale blue. The outline of the sphinx appears to liquify and tremble. It expands in all directions until it is a shapeless blot of shadow, and a boy steps out of it. The wind dies down and the torches burn normally again.

The boy is, perhaps, nine or ten years old. He has skin the colour of honey and solemn brown eyes, his head has been shaved except for a topknot of black hair, and he wears a white shift around his waist.

Crispin finds the newcomer oddly familiar. At first he cannot place where he could have met the boy before, then he realizes that this is the person he has been seeing hidden in his mother's ghost.

'Swipe me!' cries Crispin. 'Who are you, mate?'

'This is Satepihu, the son whose throat was slit by his father Imhotep,' Anubis says. 'This is the soul Imhotep trapped inside the sphinx to make his magic, the

285

soul you were born to set free, heathen boy.'

Crispin and Satepihu regard each other. There is gratitude in Satepihu's eyes, and he smiles a smile that is open and friendly enough to span scores of centuries.

Crispin returns the smile, just as Squalida says, 'And now that Crispin Rattle has passed his test, can we go home?'

Anubis laughs his appalling laugh.

'In a while,' he says. 'There is a matter that must be attended to first. Show yourself, unfaithful servant!'

The sound of clopping is heard coming from one of the doorways, and a demon enters the chamber. Its face and chest are cherry red, its pointed chin is tufted with black whiskers, and ram's horns coil at its temples. From the waist down, the demon has the hindquarters of a pied bull, with a long and slender tail that flicks and lashes.

There are, doubtless, countless demons

who are identical, but Callisto instantly recognizes this individual and steps forward as he shouts its name, 'Bazimaal!'

Bazimaal lifts its hand and a force comes out of its palm that sets the air rippling like heat-shimmer, and sends Callisto sprawling.

'Not today, Callisto,' Bazimaal says with a leer. 'If our story has an end, it's somewhere in the future.' To Anubis, Bazimaal says, 'Have I achieved what you asked of me, Lord Anubis?'

'Your ancient debt to me is now discharged and the time of your servitude is over,' Anubis says. He snarls at Jasper. 'You trapped this drivelling fool and deceived him into bringing the Black Sphinx back to light. You are free to return to your native realm, Bazimaal. Leave this world and do not return to it.'

Bazimaal licks its lips with its black tongue.

'I wonder if you'd grant me the slightest

of favours before I go, Lord Anubis,' it says. 'When you've finished with Jasper here, can I have what remains of him?'

'When I have done with him, nothing will remain,' says Anubis.

'Oh dear! And I had such plans for him!' sighs Bazimaal.

The torchlight blinks like an eyelid, and the demon is no longer there.

Anubis breathes in Jasper's face and says, 'Some final words perhaps, fool?'

Jasper considers making a clean breast of it and confessing to all the crimes that he is guilty of, but the list is far too long to bear recitation, and besides, he is quite insane.

'I do not acknowledge that you have any authority over me in this matter, Anubis,' he blusters. 'You have treated me shoddily, stolen a valuable piece of my property and transformed it into a worthless child. I know my rights – don't think I don't – and I insist upon an interview with your superior this instant.'

Anubis throws back his head and howls, 'Come forth, Amenuit, Devourer of Unworthy Souls!'

A shape emerges from the doorway to Jasper's right, and what a shape it is. The monstrous Amenuit has the jaws of a crocodile, the mane and claws of a lion and the rump of a hippopotamus, attached to a body that is dog-like. He is impossibly agile, shockingly cruel and insatiably hungry.

Jasper Pepper appreciates now why Destiny is also known as 'Doom' and his face turns ashen.

'Ah!' he says. 'This puts rather a different complexion on things. I may have given you the wrong impression, Lord Anubis. Surely we can talk over our unfortunate misunderstanding and come to some form of agreement?'

'End him!' Anubis says to Amenuit.

Amenuit springs. His claws rip, his teeth tear.

Bones crunch, sinews crack, blood splashes.

Jasper Pepper warbles out a wail of agony as Amenuit takes off his left leg, just below the knee, and crocodiles it down.

Crispin is horrified and fascinated. He cannot bear to watch, neither can he look away, but he is saved from further nightmarish scenes. Like the pother from a smoking oil-lamp, the walls of Squalida MacHeath's room waver around him, and then solidify. He finds that he is clutching Aril's hand, and he releases it with an embarrassed cough. On the opposite side of the room, Callisto stands up and dusts himself off.

Squalida MacHeath goes straight to her occasional table, pops the cork of the bottle and pours herself a glass of champagne, draining it in a single gulp.

'Mr Callisto,' she says, 'despite reports to the contrary, I am basically a woman who likes her life to be uncomplicated, and you have complicated it beyond recognition. I don't know how you managed to do what you did – nor do I wish to know. All that concerns me is my good name among the criminal fraternity. No one gets the better of Squalida MacHeath, not even demons and gods. If you, or any of your friends, dare to speak a word of my part in what took place tonight, I shall be forced to—'

'I would never be so ill-mannered as to take a lady's name in vain, Miss MacHeath,' Callisto assures her. 'You may depend upon our absolute discretion.'

'And who'd believe us if we told them?' adds Crispin.

Callisto retrieves a gold watch from a pocket in his waistcoat and glances at it.

'As I suspected, time is of a different order in the Land of the Dead,' he says. 'Our sojourn there lasted no more than two earthly minutes.'

Squalida arranges herself on her chaise longue and yawns.

'I don't know about you lot, but I could sleep like an enchanted princess,' she says.

'Then Crispin, Aril and I should take our leave,' says Callisto. 'It hasn't exactly been a pleasure to meet you, Miss MacHeath, but—'

'You wouldn't mind meeting me again under different circumstances?' Squalida suggests. 'Well, you never know your luck, Mr Callisto.'

But the sparkle in her eyes tells Callisto precisely what his luck might be.

ƐPILOGUƐ

When Callisto, Aril, Crispin and Mrs Moncrief are reunited outside St Augustine's, it is an occasion for much celebration and one or two tears of relief. Then it is back to Scarlatti Mews. Three makes for a tight fit in a hansom cab, but Callisto, Aril and Crispin manage it somehow.

Crispin remains confused.

'Mr Callisto,' he says, 'can you explain about that kid to me, and what the dog bloke said?'

He is also curious about Bazimaal and Amenuit, but first things first.

'You may recall that Professor Lyons

mentioned that the Vizier Imhotep sacrificed his own son to make the Black Sphinx,' says Callisto. 'The boy's soul was bound inside the figure. Anubis alone could free the soul, but only if the sphinx was brought to him by someone innocent, unselfish and courageous. That person was you, Crispin. It was the sphinx's fate to become the possession of the corrupt and the evil – until it came to you. The boy you saw was the soul set free at last, and now he will walk for ever in the Country of Bliss.'

'But the dog bloke said that the sphinx chose me before I was born!' Crispin explains. 'How's that then?'

Callisto shrugs.

'Sometimes the workings of ancient magic are too deep to fathom,' he says. 'But the Black Sphinx is no more, Jasper Pepper is dead and our world is safe again.'

Aril wriggles into a position where she can see Callisto's face and says, 'But there's still a problem that needs to be solved.'

'And what would that be?' says Callisto.

'What are we to do with Crispin Rattle?'

'Hmm, what indeed?' says Callisto. 'I've been thinking for a while that my stage performances might be enhanced by a second assistant, preferably a boy. Such a boy would need to be accommodated, and the back parlour, suitably redecorated and refurbished, would do admirably. A private tutor would have to be hired to see to his education. The boy would be expected to study diligently, lend a hand with chores about the house, and be especially polite to Mrs Moncrief. I would also consider making him privy to some of the secrets of conjuring.'

'Have you any particular boy in mind?' enquires Aril.

She and Callisto look at Crispin, and smile.

'What – me?' yelps Crispin. 'Stop with you in Scarlatti Mews and never go back to London no more? That *is* prodigious!'

Each chapter of this dastardly and blood-soaked book contains a verse of the Black Sphinx's curse. Be prepared to unleash its tyranny – decode it at your peril! And beware of the Devourer of Souls!

Think you've cracked it? Go to www.**kids**at**randomhouse**.co.uk/sphinx to find out, and attempt more cryptic mind-bogglers!!

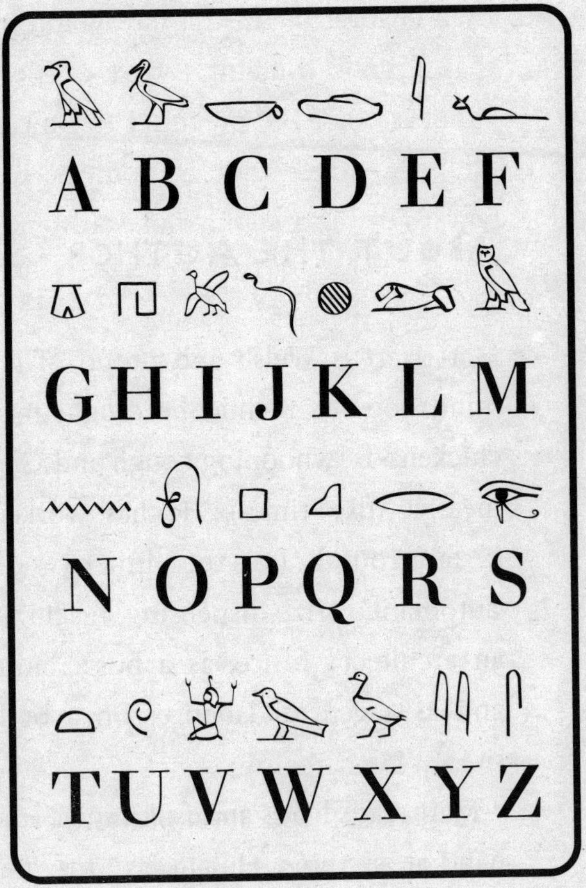
A B C D E F
G H I J K L M
N O P Q R S
T U V W X Y Z

ABOUT THE AUTHOR

Matt Hart is Welsh and proud of it – so mind now. As a child he caught measles, chickenpox, whooping cough and German measles (five times). He has worked on a fairground (as the innards of an 'automatic' prize-dispensing machine), in an architect's office, as a bus conductor, and as a general labourer on a building site.

Matt reads loads and isn't much of a dab hand at anything. He always looks untidy, even when he's wearing expensive clothes. His favourite animal is the coati-mundi.

Matt is married and lives in Berkshire.